Samuel Wilson

George Paull of Benita, West Africa

A memoir

Samuel Wilson

George Pauli of Benita, West Africa
A memoir

ISBN/EAN: 9783337308698

Printed in Europe, USA, Canada, Australia, Japan

Cover: Foto ©Raphael Reischuk / pixelio.de

More available books at **www.hansebooks.com**

GEORGE PAULL,

OF

BENITA, WEST AFRICA.

A MEMOIR.

BY THE
Rev. SAMUEL WILSON, D.D.

PHILADELPHIA:
PRESBYTERIAN BOARD OF PUBLICATION,
No. 1334 Chestnut Street.

WESTCOTT & THOMSON,
Stereotypers and Electrotypers, Philada.

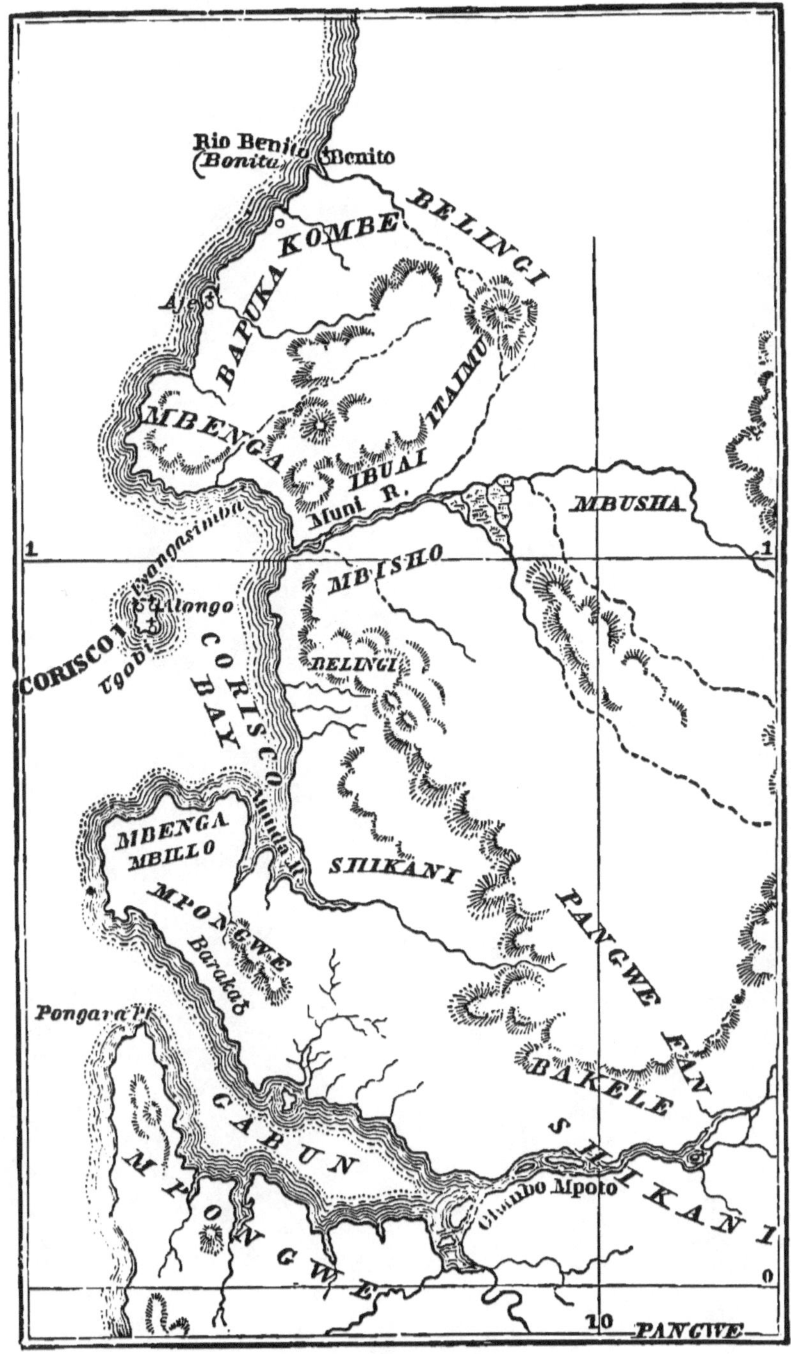

GABOON AND CORISCO.

PREFACE.

Those who would know something of Africa, and of the life, labors and privations of our devoted missionaries in that dark land, will, we trust, find a deep interest in perusing this memoir of one whom God has greatly honored, but early called to his rest and reward. As his heart burned with the love of the gospel and the cause of Christian missions, though dead, he may yet speak to those who are the hope of the Church to fulfill her mission to a perishing world. The volume has been prepared mainly for the *young*, and our earnest prayer is that God's blessing may rest on all who read it. It consists chiefly of Mr. Paull's letters, written to relatives and intimate friends with the usual freedom and familiarity of correspondence, and without the remotest idea of their publication.

GEORGE PAULL.

GEORGE PAULL was the second son of Joseph and Eliza Lea Paull, and was born near Connellsville, a beautiful and romantic village on the banks of the Youghiogheny River, in Fayette County, Pa., Feb. 3, 1837. His boyhood, like that of many of Pennsylvania's noblest sons, was spent on his father's farm. His early education was largely in the common and Sabbath-schools, but especially around the domestic altar, from which the incense of the morning and evening sacrifice ascended— the place where young hearts are prepared for Christian and missionary work.

Full of youthful ardor and enterprise, with his elder brother and other companions George often sported on the rugged banks of Dunbar Creek, and the craggy steeps of the Laurel Mountain, adjacent to his lovely home. Here he drank health from the mountain breezes, and vigorous thoughts and imaginations from the bold scenery which on every hand greeted his eye. While his young life was thus being developed into manhood, God was preparing him, by faithful teachings and fervent prayers, for a higher life of spiritual consecration.

Children are God's heritage, and he calls and qualifies them for his service. For this he puts into operation fitting instrumentalities. Chief among these are the family altar, the Sabbath-school and the church. To all these George evinced an early and strong attachment. He was an earnest pupil in the Sabbath-school and Bible-class, often taking the prize for good conduct and successful recitations. Being of a modest and generous disposition, these honors were cheerfully accorded to him by all. In church he was always an attentive and profited hearer of the word of life. Thus he grew in knowledge as in stature.

He commenced classical and mathematical studies under the Rev. R. Stevenson, pastor of the Presbyterian church at Connellsville, continued them in Dunlap's Creek Presbyterian Academy, and afterwards under Prof. John Frazer, from Cromarty, Scotland, the successful wrangler for the Huttonian prize in the University of St. Andrews—for a time president of the Royal College in the Bermu-

EARLY HOME.

p. 7.

das, and afterwards professor of mathematics in Jefferson College, Pa.—a teacher of high qualifications. With such preparatory training, young Paull, with his older brother, A. Torrence Paull, entered Jefferson College at Canonsburg, where he graduated with high credit in the class of 1858, in the twenty-first year of his age.

Though he frequently had seasons of deep concern about his spiritual state and prospects, it was not till the spring of 1858, during a revival of religion in the college, that he obtained a hope in Christ and made a public profession of religion, which he did in the church at Connellsville, of which his father is a ruling elder.

After leaving college, Mr. Paull went to Mississippi and taught for a short time. But realizing his call of God to preach Christ, he returned and entered the Western Theological Seminary at Allegheny, Pa., where he spent three years diligently preparing for his great life work of preaching Christ to the heathen. The love of Christ, and a burning desire to save those sitting in utter darkness, fired his heart and inspired his daily meditations and prayers for divine direction. In April, 1861, at the outbreak of our terrible civil war, he was, by the Presbytery of Redstone, licensed to preach the gospel of grace and good will to men. In April, 1862, he completed his course in the seminary.

Fully realizing his call of God to the missionary work in the foreign field, he offered his name to the General Assembly's Board of Foreign Missions for the work in Africa, and was accepted. But on account of the embarrassed condition of the Board, arising from the civil war, he could not be sent on his mission immediately. For a time he supplied Tyrone and Sewickley churches, then without a pastor, where he is affectionately remembered as the devout and earnest preacher whose sole aim was to bring sinners to Christ. At the suggestion of the author, he went to the West and found a vacant, scattered church at Morrison, Illinois, in the Presbytery of Rock River, to which he ministered with great popularity and success. From their earnest entreaties to become their pastor, he found it difficult to tear himself away to obey the call of God to preach the gospel to poor benighted Africa. When his devoted friends at Morrison gathered around him, and besought him with tears to abide with them in the pastoral work, his spirit was sorely tried. But his sense of duty to Christ and the perishing heathen prevailed. He was ordained an evangelist for the missionary work, by the Presbytery of Redstone, in October, 1863.

Mr. Paull was regarded by all who knew him as a Christian and minister of rare piety and promise. As a son, he was affectionately devoted to his parents, who early dedicated him to God in Christian baptism, and prayerfully nurtured him in the doctrines and duties of religion. As a friend, he was remarkably ingenuous and constant. As a student, he was conscientious, diligent and successful, beloved and admired by his companions and teachers. His scholarship was highly respectable; his understanding was comprehensive; his imagination fertile and chaste; his memory good, and his taste refined. His reading and observation were not so extensive as they were judicious and profitable, of the kind best adapted to qualify him for his cherished work of preaching "Christ and him crucified."

His piety was peculiarly simple and artless, deep, earnest and practical. It was of that lovely type which distinguished the beloved disciple. His large heart was an utter stranger to the spirit of selfishness and censoriousness, and his lips to the speech of unkindness; but both were familiar with thoughts and expressions of goodness. Emptied of self, he clung to Christ and his righteousness with most affectionate devotion. He felt bound, in covenant fidelity, by earnest prayer and self-examination to find daily experience in his inner life that would attest the gracious indwelling of the Holy Spirit; hence, he would call himself to account before God, and confess his sins and shortcomings in duty with deep humiliation of spirit. This is seen in his letters and diary of missionary labors and spiritual life in Africa. Active and laborious beyond his physical strength, full of holy zeal and charity, he was ever elaborating schemes of usefulness. The burden of the Lord on his heart continually was, that he and others might be fully awake to their high responsibility in working, praying and giving for Christ and the salvation of the perishing in all lands. Few men of his age have evinced such weanedness from the world and devotion to Christ, such wakeful, tireless sympathy with all efforts to sow the seeds of salvation beside all waters, even to the remotest parts of the pagan world.

As a preacher, Mr. Paull was, in the best sense, eminently popular. His preaching was scriptural, pungent, tender, earnest, practical and faithful. His aim was not the mere entertainment of his hearers, but their conversion and sanctification through the truth, which he pressed, like the sainted McCheyne, in such winning and cogent strains that young and old would congregate in crowds to hear him.

Of a portly and commanding presence, with a deep, full and wonderfully sweet and persuasive voice, fervent and eloquent in sentiment, logical and forcible in argument, natural and striking in his illustrations, and withal filled with love to Christ and the souls of men, he never failed to stamp his burning thoughts on the hearts of his audience and win souls to Jesus. Who that heard his sermons on Christian missions can ever forget their ardent spirit and melting power as he pleaded for the cause of Christ among the heathen? He seemed to verify that tender of personal agency, "Here am I, send me." Although his popular talents and manners seemed to mark out for him a ministerial career in some large city church, yet his self-denying spirit and zeal for the salvation of the destitute determined him to one of the humblest and most perilous of all the fields of missionary work—a missionary to Africa. Now that his work is quickly done, and the Master has called him to the unfading crown, the Church might well inscribe on the beautiful marble monument erected to his memory by parental affection in the cemetery at Corisco, as her estimate of his character, "By the grace of God, a bright example of devotion to the missionary work." This noble standard-bearer having fallen, the Church looks earnestly to see his likeness reproduced in some of her sons, who shall seize and bear the banner onward to final victory in reclaiming Africa for Christ. But let us permit him to speak for himself, and in his familiar letters and the brief notes of his diary tell the story of his missionary life.

On his arrival at New York, on his way to Africa, Mr. Paull wrote to his parents:

New York, Nov. 27, 1863.

"To-night I am in Astoria, at the house of Dr. Lowrie. I arrived to-day at noon, went to the mission-house, met Mr. Rankin and Dr. Lowrie, also Mr. and Mrs. Clark, missionaries to Africa. Secured a passage in the steamer 'City of London' for Liverpool. The vessel sails to-morrow at noon, and I leave America perhaps for many a day; but there is no sadness in it to me, for I look beyond, I hope. Instead of sailing from Liverpool, I am to sail from Glasgow, Scotland, as that is the port to which the vessel belongs. So after sailing to Liverpool, I go to Glasgow, and it is possible I may have to be there for a considerable time. The steamer on which I go to Liverpool is one of the very best, so that you need have no uneasiness on that score. I do not think you can hear from me again until I reach Liverpool, when I hope to write to you at some length. Good-bye till then, and may the blessing of our heavenly Father rest on you all."

Again, he writes to them from on board of the steamer "City of London":

"Dec. 7, 1863.

"Many a league from shore to-day, we are steaming on the broad Atlantic, but by noon on to-morrow, if Providence favor, we hope to reach the harbor of Cork, Ireland, and thence about a day will bring us to Liverpool. Our voyage thus far has been most prosperous, speedy and pleasant—fair winds and favoring tides all the way. On account of the heavy fog on Saturday, 28th, we did not get out of New York harbor until Sabbath morning; we left the wharf at 7 A. M., and sailed down the channel, with Staten Island on our right and Long Island on our left. Passing the three or four bristling forts for the defence of the harbor, and the 'lightship,' as it is called—a ship that always stands anchored in the bay, and is lit up at night as a landmark to the proper channel—and, passing out of Sandy Hook, we dropped our pilot and soon were out of sight of land. The passengers (about thirty-five or forty) nearly all gathered on deck, for the sake of the fresh air, and there with busy tread they passed to and fro, in hopes of driving away all symptoms of the dreaded sea-sickness, but it was a useless expedient; sea-sickness would come; and ere long one of our gentlemen, a State Senator from New Jersey, grew suddenly pale, and hurried off to the railing at the stern of the vessel, and we saw but little more of him for several days. Many more of my fellow-passengers, from time to time, slipped off more quietly to their state-rooms, there to roll about in misery for almost half the voyage. All of the passengers are about now and able to appear at table, but some of them look pale and a little thin. You are anxious to know, I suppose, how I came through this general *epidemic*. Unexpectedly to myself (but I can scarcely say that, for I did not really expect to be much sick), I had but little of it. I felt a little nausea for a few days, and once or twice *was relieved of my supper*, but generally I had a good appetite and was in my seat at the table, and now I am as comfortable as the land could make me.

"This is the ninth day out from New York. The weather, generally, since we started has been quite pleasant, one or two days very bright and sunny. We have no variety of scenery here; every day, in respect to that, is alike: a large circular basin of dashing waves, expanding far as the eye can reach and meeting the horizon, is the scenery for one day and for all. The waves do not seem very high, from the deck of the vessel, but they are rolling and dashing against each other, sometimes, too, breaking clear over the bulwarks of the vessel. We have not seen a vessel since we left New York, nor anything that has life, save the sea-gulls, that constantly follow in our wake in large numbers, picking up the crumbs and waste that are thrown overboard. They are a beautiful bird as they skim around and over the deck of the vessel. They are about the size of *pigeons*, white, all except their backs and the tops of their wings. Sometimes at night the waters present a beautiful sight, as the vessel ploughs through them and rolls them back all sparkling and bright as though filled with electric sparks.

"I have been very fortunate in getting a good

steamer for crossing the ocean; everything about it is in superb order. It is the newest of the Philadelphia, New York and Liverpool line, which runs regularly and carries the mail between New York and Liverpool. It is an iron-plated steamer, most substantially built at the cost of half a million of dollars. Officers and stewards are very gentlemanly and polite, all of them Englishmen. I could give you no idea of the appearance of an ocean steamer, unless it be that it looks like an immense black boat with a deck rising up inside of it a few feet higher than its sides, and on top of this are the three masts and sails. Under the deck is the cabin, about one hundred feet long and forty wide; in it the passengers sit and take their meals. The next story below the cabin is filled up with state-rooms, all fitted up most comfortably. I have one to myself. Under the state-rooms is the hold, which is used for freight, etc.

"Life on board the vessel is very dull and lazy. Most of the passengers lounge around on the cushioned seats that run all around the cabin, reading or talking or dozing, feeling too unsettled both in *stomach* and mind to undertake anything that would require much energy. We have breakfast every morning at 9 o'clock, lunch at 12 o'clock, dinner at 4 o'clock, and tea at $6\frac{1}{2}$ o'clock. Our dinners are generally sumptuous, consisting of four or five courses, and requiring about one hour and a half to get through them: first course soups— ox-tail, clam or mock-turtle; then meats and fowls of all kinds, prepared in almost every way; then cheese and celery; then pastry, pies, puddings, tarts, etc.; then fruits, apples, oranges, figs, raisins, almonds, English walnuts, etc. This is a pretty sumptuous bill of fare, but it will not be long until we shall be able to change this style of living for something plainer.

"Our passengers are all pleasant and genteel. They are a mixed company of English, Scotch, Canadians, French and Americans, Protestants, Roman Catholics and infidels, one honorable, two or three sea-captains, and the rest I believe are private individuals. Among the captains (who are all blockade-runners) are two who were taken about Wilmington. One commanded the Robert Lee, which was captured, and the other the Venus, which was burned. Seven or eight of our passengers are ladies. One lost her husband and her only child on this vessel as it came over to New York the last time, and now she is going back again in it to her home, desolate enough. I like the young Senator from New Jersey very much. Presbyterian proclivities brought us together. His father was a Presbyterian minister, and his brother is one also, and is now settled in Springfield, Ohio. The one with whom I am most intimate is a young merchant from New York, who attends Dr. Phillips' church. Dr. Lowrie introduced me to him just as we were going aboard. He has often been across the ocean, and I find it an immense advantage to have such an acquaintance. He seems to be a very modest, noble fellow.

"We had service on board yesterday (Sabbath)— Church of England service—in the morning, read by the captain, as is the rule of the ship; and I preached in the afternoon at 1 o'clock. I had a very pleasant little audience, and preached with a good deal of satisfaction, though it was difficult to keep steadily on my feet, as the vessel rolls all the time. Indeed, it is a pretty difficult matter to write, and I hope this will excuse the more than usual *unreadableness* of my letter.

"The apples and cakes which Lizzie deposited in my trunk I fetched out a few nights since, and found them all very nice, more especially so as they had the flavor of *home*. Everything that suggests home is pleasant to the taste or sight. It was a sore pang to part with all that I hold dear on earth, and yet I feel sure that it is of the Lord, and I rejoice exceedingly that he has called me and given me grace to do even this little for him. My days, I think, are now as happy as almost any that I have ever spent, in prospect of the work that God has called me to do, and that he has conferred this great favor on me—sending me to the heathen to tell the story of Christ and the cross. I have no doubt in regard to the fulfillment of that promise to those that forsake father and mother, etc. I trust that I can now lay claim to it, and I am assured that Christ will be to me more than all earthly things.

" There is a gentleness and kindness in Dr. Lowrie's manner very attractive. He and his father made me a present of four or five books before I came away—Walter Lowrie's ' Memoirs and Sermons,' etc. He and Mr. Rankin, Mr. Waugh, and Mr. Beatty of New Brunswick, came down with me to the ship to see me off. Mr. Waugh promised to drop you a letter to say that I got off safely, as you could not hear from me again until I arrived at Liverpool.

" *Tuesday,* Dec. 8.—This morning, for the first time since leaving New York, we saw the land again, and right glad we all were. Sailing up the Irish channel, just to our left lay *Old Ireland.* Its rugged shores looked bleak and barren enough at the distance of two or three miles, but when we drew nearer they looked better. At Queenstown, the harbor of Cork (about twelve o'clock), we stopped long enough to send off some of our passengers by a *tug* which steamed up to us. The shores looked green and all hedged off into little fields. On the hillside we saw a flock of goats quietly browsing. The houses seemed a good deal lower than ours, apparently built of stone, and roofed with thatch. On the other side of us was an island on which the Irish keep their convicts.

" To-day it is gloomy and drizzling, but not cold, nor has it been since we left. A good deal of fog is still hanging over us as we steam up the Irish Channel, and now night has come on ; but by 9 or 10 o'clock to-morrow we hope to be in Liverpool. An old captain on board tells me that this will be the quickest trip ever made by a screw steamer. I saw a sailor-boy climb to the mast head, one hundred and fifty feet above deck. They are a merry set of fellows. They work their ropes to a song, and good music they make of it. I shall not have time to write in the morning, so I will close to-night, and mail my letter from Liverpool to-morrow. I may go to Glasgow by way of London, and will of course write to you again from Glasgow. A great deal of love to each member of the family, and may the richest blessings of our Father in heaven rest on you all."

"London, Dec. 12, 1863.

"My Dear Sister: As you see, I am in the *great city* to-night, and have already spent two or three days here seeing the wonders of England's great capital.

"My last letter I wrote at sea and mailed in Liverpool. I hope it reached you in due time. When I landed at Liverpool, I found that I had several days before the vessel was to sail from Glasgow for Africa, and so I concluded to pay a visit to London. My baggage I sent on to Glasgow by a clever young Scotchman of Glasgow, with whom I became acquainted on board the vessel.

"We landed safely at Liverpool on Wednesday morning, had our baggage examined, but the examination really amounted to nothing. Mr. Thorp and I footed it from there up to the railway dépôt for London, stopping on the way at the Liverpool Exchange, which is said to be much more magnificent than the great London Exchange. Both of them are immense, massive stone buildings, supported on great columns. Within the courts are scores of burly brokers and speculators of every description, chattering and chaffering and striking bargains. I visited also St. George's Hall, in which they hold their courts, etc. It also is built of stone, and in magnificence and grandeur, without and within, it far surpasses anything I had ever seen before. Indeed, when standing before it, as well as before many other buildings I have since seen, I have been dumb with amazement, and feel utterly unable to give a description of them. I started for London the same evening about 4 o'clock, and was hurried along at almost lightning speed until about 9 o'clock, when we found ourselves landed in the midst of cabs and cabmen at the London dépôt—distance over two hundred miles. In company with some others I took a cab and went to the Terminus Hotel, at the end of the great London bridge, a good hotel and of very moderate charges. Their hotel system here is very different from ours. For instance, we paid two shillings (half a dollar) for room and bed, and then we could take our meals wherever we liked. It is much cheaper and as pleasant to get them at some coffee-house. A mutton chop and cup of coffee for breakfast, at about a shil-

ling; and a mutton chop here is almost equal to a
dish of oysters in point of delicacy—so rich and
juicy. We do not know anything about them in
America. On Thursday morning, Mr. Greenly (a
young man who came over with us in the vessel)
and I started out to see the sights. St. Paul's
Cathedral was the first object of interest to which
we bent our steps. So, passing down by the pier
of London Bridge to the river Thames—and
London Bridge, by the way, deserves a word, it has
so great a fame; but it is not imposing in appearance. There is no wood, no wire, no paint about it:
all stone and mortar. The arches beneath, and the
side walls running up four or five feet from the floor,
and the floor paved with stone just like the street,
is all that there is of it. But then London Bridge
is such a wonderful thoroughfare. In the after-
noons it is a strange sight to see the pell-mell rush
of wagons, cabs, omnibuses, all mixed up and moving to and fro as best they can, and footmen in the
same dilemma.

" But to St. Paul's we took a boat at the *pier*—
little tugs that steam up and down the river with
wonderful rapidity, carrying passengers at a penny
apiece to any distance almost — and ran up to
the St. Paul's wharf, and from that a short walk

brought us to the cathedral. But of that grand old pile of stone, rising upward toward the clouds more than four hundred feet, I can scarcely say anything that would be satisfactory. You would think me wonderfully enthusiastic if I should attempt to speak anything as I feel in regard to it. Entering by the north door, you are at once in the main and central part, an immense amphitheatre, in which you might place almost a score of churches, steeples and all. All around this vast dome, on the walls and against them and against the columns, are monuments and sculptures with inscriptions to the memory of the great dead—generally their full-length effigies carved in marble. You look up, and about three hundred feet above you, all around the inside of the dome, are splendid paintings illustrative of incidents in Scripture. From the floor, by paying two shillings, you are taken by guides to the very crown (a flight of over six hundred steps), and a weary climb it is. Your first landing-place is on the 'First Gallery,' about two hundred feet high on the outside; the next is the 'Golden Gallery,' about one hundred feet higher, and from here one can see all over London. But the day was foggy. Greenly and I, as most others do, climbed on until we stuck our heads up into the inside of the topmost crown. Of course there was no danger, as it is all inside of the building. We then came down and looked at the clock, which is about two hundred years old, and reminds you of a small saw-mill running several circular saws. Then we gave a glance at the library and the *great bell* and the circular stairway, which are all well worth a careful survey. It really seems as if it were worth a trip across the Atlantic to peep into St. Paul's.

"In the vaults below, through which we also went, lie the bones of those who died centuries ago, and some of later date, as the Duke of Wellington and Lord Nelson, I think, and Benjamin West, the great artist from our own land (Pennsylvania). Never lived there a man in Great Britain, I suppose, whose memory is so revered as that of the Duke of Wellington. Near to his tomb, which is a splendid mausoleum, is deposited the car on which he was drawn by ten black horses to his last resting-place. It is a splendid and costly affair; the wheels (twelve in number) are all brass, moulded from the cannon which, I think, he captured at Waterloo. The body of the car is covered with black cloth, adorned with trappings and immense ostrich plumes. Around the walls of

the vault are hung black cloth and trappings and
armor. The vault is lit up by candles constantly
kept burning.

"After spending some hours thus most pleasantly in St. Paul's, we dined, and went to visit
the Houses of Parliament. These, too, are very
gorgeous. They are just across the street from
the old Westminster Abbey. Entering at the
door and passing through an immense hall, high
and arched, we ascended a few steps and then entered another hall to the left. Each side of this
hall was lined with full-length statues of England's
great ones—Pitt and Grattan and others. At the
end of this hall, right and left, are the House of
Commons and the House of Lords. I went into
the House of Commons, but I cannot describe its
gorgeousness. The House of Lords was closed, and
visitors were not admitted except on Saturdays.
But by permission of one of the police, who are
always in attendance, I got into a hall from which,
through a glass door, I could get a peep at its
magnificence. The throne, on which her majesty
sits when she presides, was covered over, so that I
did not get a sight of it. The Houses of Parliament are right on the bank of the river Thames.

" We next passed over to the great Westminster

Abbey, memorable in English history for many a century. Parts of it yet remain in the old Saxon and Norman style of architecture. Beneath its pavements lie the bones of many a monk interred before the Reformation, some of them eight or nine hundred years ago. Here all of England's kings and queens have been crowned for many a generation; and here also lie their bones. The whole building is an immense affair, splendidly adorned with all that the sculptor's chisel, in times both ancient and modern, could supply. Many of the windows are filled with the most beautiful Scriptural designs, painted on the glass. Here I stood on the graves of Addison (of the Spectator) and Southey and Johnson and Garrick and Sheridan and Campbell and Spenser. Macaulay, too, lay near by, and many others of the noble dead. They lie just under the stone floor; some of them have slabs lying over them, and almost all have busts and inscriptions to their memory on the wall. I stood, too, beside the tomb of Queen Elizabeth, for whose memory (although she was a great queen) I do not have any wonderful respect. Mary, Queen of Scots, whom she so hated in life, lies near her in death, and I stood beside her vault, on top of which is her full-length statue, recumbent.

"In one of the chapels I was shown the *stone chair* on which the monarchs of England are crowned, and have been for a long time back. It looks old and rusty, and seems to have been cut out of solid stone. On one side of the Abbey is an entrance for the royal family, along which no others are allowed to tread. In one part of the Abbey, service is kept up twice a day all the year round—the service of the Established Church, the same as the Episcopal Church in America, with the exception of some little formalities, viz., bowing the head whenever the name of Christ is mentioned; chanting their prayers; having their choirs composed of little boys in white robes. I have not seen any of the royal family since I have been in London, nor any of the nobility, as they are all out of the city.

"English people, so far as I have met with them, seem to be very kind, noble-hearted and polite. If you ask for information on the street, or anywhere, from the highest class, they are all attention, and seem willing and anxious to do you all the kindness in their power. I think they feel kindly toward Americans, and wish Americans to feel so toward them. On every hand they say, 'When are you going to get through with this war?* It is a terrible pity to have so much blood shed.' But they will admit that the North could not well do otherwise than she has done.

"Englishmen recognize Americans almost as soon as they speak, and some of them take a great pride in it, and soon give you to understand that they know where you are from. Their accent and the pronunciation of some of their words is quite different from ours, so I am sure there would be no trouble in recognizing an Englishman anywhere.

"But to return to our travel around the city. After leaving Westminster we took a hansom—a gig which is the most common conveyance here, a heavy-wheeled affair with one horse, the driver sitting on a seat on the top behind—and drove around by St. James' Park and Buckingham Palace, which is fine, very fine indeed, but yet not so imposing as might be expected for the residence of England's Queen; and then, passing first Hyde Park, down through Temple Bar—which is an arched gateway, once the outward entrance to the city when it was walled—past St. Paul's and over London Bridge to the Terminus Hotel. But enough of description for this time. I shall not get off from Glasgow for Africa until the first of January. If I had

* The civil war then unhappily raging in the United States.

known this, I might have had the pleasure of staying longer at home. But God has ordered it as it is for the best, and I am content, as I trust I ever shall be when I walk in the way in which God leads me. I am happy, though I have a strange feeling of being cut off from the sweets of home and friends, a wayfarer, a stranger, journeying slowly onward, I trust, toward the heavenly City of which the Lord God hath said, 'I will give it thee.' I am expecting to take the morning train for Glasgow, to await the sailing of the vessel for Africa."

Mr. Paull writes his first letter from Scotland to his two younger brothers:

"Glasgow, Dec. 21, 1863.

"For nearly a week I have been snugly and pleasantly settled in this old but thriving city of the Scots. Look at the map, and you will find it on the banks of the Clyde, a little river, and once of not much note; but latterly its channel has been deepened, so that the largest vessels now sail up to the city. To this it owes its present wonderful prosperity." After a brief description of the city, he says: "On my arrival at Glasgow, last Tuesday night, I stopped at the Queen's Hotel, and a very fine one it is. While I think of it, I must tell you of some Highlanders that I saw there. They were the largest and finest-looking men that I have seen. Their dress was the peculiar part. First, a short coat extending down below the waist, then, fastened under that, and extending down to the knees, was a petticoat—'kilt' they call it. Their stockings reached up nearly to their knees, and this was their full dress—no pants on—so you may imagine there was a good opportunity for the wind to whistle about them on a cold day, for their legs were entirely bare except the clothing I have mentioned. They were officers of a Highland regiment in the British army, and this is their usual dress.

"Next morning I went to hunt up Mr. Laughland, in whose ship I am to go out. He was not in, but one of his clerks, who has spent some years on the coast of Africa, asked me if I was Mr. Paull, and said that a Mr. Thompson, who had been a missionary on the coast of Africa at Calabar, and was now at home recruiting his health, at his uncle's house, wanted to see me. The clerk took me down to call on him, and they so insisted on my making my home with them that I could not refuse without being rude. So here I am, feeling perfectly at home, and receiving every kindness, in this warm-hearted Scotch family. The family consists of the missionary and his sister (a young lady), an uncle and aunt, both unmarried. They are all pleasant, and great friends to the missionaries. They seem to make it a point to entertain all missionaries who come along this way.

" Mr. Thompson's station is a few hundred miles north of that to which I go. I met also a missionary and his wife just starting out to Calabar. It seems to be a short trip from here to Africa, a good many missionaries going and returning, and young men going out as clerks and traders along the coast. I find I am not likely to get off before the middle of January. The ship is not yet returned from the coast, but is expected about New Year. It will then be to load and repair."

Mr. Paull resumes his report of sights in London, and says: " I found my way to the British Museum, and there, in that wonderful collection of natural history (nor are works of art by any means wanting), I spent most of the day. It is a great building, covering perhaps an acre or two, with immense rooms hundreds of feet long, running in every direction, and these filled with collections of every kind, from every clime. Going up stairs, almost the first things that I saw were Du

Chaillu's gorillas, three of them (stuffed, of course), and one of them an immense creature. There were stuffed elephants, rhinoceroses, giraffes, lions, bears, deer, antelope, and every kind of animal you could mention, and hundreds of animals which you have never seen, nor even heard their names. In the departments for the birds, I suppose I may safely say there were tens of thousands of stuffed specimens, of every size and shape and color, from almost every clime under the sun. In the department for reptiles it was the same—alligators, lizards, snakes, seals, the walrus, etc. There was also a department for geological collections which was very interesting—the bones of animals dug from the earth after having been buried for ages; rocks of different kinds, with every possible impression of plants and animals and reptiles on them. There were also departments for the antiquities that have been found in the ancient cities. Layard's discoveries are there from Nineveh, etc. Also mummies from Egypt, mummied cats and mummied dogs. Also sarcophagi from Greece and Rome, Indian curiosities, and curiosities from Greenland and Iceland—clothes of skin, sledges, etc. Besides these, they have vast libraries containing thousands upon thousands of volumes, and also autograph letters and manuscripts by the great men of the world for many centuries back. I saw the original will of Mary, Queen of Scots, and the prayer-book which Lady Jane Grey used on the scaffold ; some of the writings of Milton and Addison, written with their own hands. It would be impossible to give you a description of the things that are there, and, even if it could be done, it would not be very satisfactory. But I hope you may one day be able to see them for yourselves. Good-bye. Give much love to all; and that you may be noble and faithful boys is the prayer of your brother."

To his parents he writes:

"GLASGOW, Dec. 29, 1863.

" From old habit, I suppose, I feel that I ought always to be at least doing something toward writing you a letter every week. Those I have already mailed since I landed on this side of the water I trust have duly come to hand. My thoughts wander back and cluster around my old home with a daily constancy. But I have been kindly kept from either sadness or loneliness, so that I trust you may never have occasion to think of me in any other way than as calmly content and happy in treading the path which I trust the providence of God has marked out for me. The lines have fallen to me in pleasant places here, and, unexpectedly, I have been set down among as kind friends as I could have met with in my own land. From the very first they have taken me in and treated me with the most kind and careful attention, making me feel as perfectly at home, almost, as though I had known them all my life. The members of the family are all warm-hearted Christians, and their being so intimately interested in the missionary work, through their nephew and his father (who was also a missionary, and died away in the interior of Africa), they have a kindly sympathy for all who are wending their way to and from the heathen.

" The nephew has spent most of his life in Africa, was about fourteen or fifteen when his father died, and was with him on an expedition into the interior at the time. After his father's death, he, being the only white person in the company, took charge of the expedition back again to Sierra Leone. After this he came to Scotland for his education, and went out again as a missionary to Calabar, a few hundred miles north of Corisco. He has since then been out ten years, spending five years there, and then coming home a year or two to recruit. I hear so much of the coast of Africa that it scarcely seems to be a far-off land, and all that I have heard has but heightened my zeal for the work, and helped at least to confirm the hope that my call to go there is indeed of God.

"I have had a glimpse or two at Glasgow people at a public 'tea-party,' a peculiar institution on this side of the water. These parties are held in their large halls. I was at one last night in the City Hall, given by the Young Men's Christian Association. A shilling at the door admits you. Within, the seats are ranged alongside of narrow tables running the whole length of the hall. On these are seated a vast assemblage, awaiting the dealing out of the *popular beverage.* At the appointed hour (7 o'clock) the chairman, a tall Scotch baron, took his seat, and after a short prayer the tea-drinking commenced, and cakes of various kinds were served with it. This lasts half an hour, and the remainder of the evening is filled up with speeches, generally from the more eminent ministers of the city. The evening passed away very pleasantly. The speeches were good, generally having some bearing on the association. This custom of so much public speech-making must be a great tax on the ministers, in addition to the duties connected with their various charges ; and yet they seem in a measure obliged to take part in these things, or be lost sight of in the busy city. I was at another, in honor of the installation of Dr. Brown over one of the churches, much the same in kind as this of which I have spoken.

"You will perhaps wonder how my Christmas was spent, as I also was striving to guess how you were all enjoying yours. By previous invitation, I went to partake of a family dinner at a brother of Mr. Thompson's, in another part of the city. We dined on roast turkey and plum pudding, which is, I believe, the favorite Christmas fare with both English and Scotch. I met at the dinner a very pleasant gentleman by the name of Shields, a relative, I believe, of the Thompsons. He has since sent me an invitation from his pastor to preach for him on next Sabbath, which I agreed to do on the morning of the day. There are several eminent ministers here that I want to hear before I go away. Dr. McDuff, the author of the 'Morning and Night Watches,' is settled here; also Andrew Bonar, author of the life of McCheyne. I heard on last Sabbath Dr. Eadie, a celebrated Scotch commentator; also two other ministers of considerable note.

"The vessel (Elgiva) is expected in from the coast of Africa in a few days now, and then in about twelve days' time she will be ready to sail again. She is a new vessel, and has an excellent captain. The voyage requires about two months. A letter was received by Mr. Thompson this morning from Mr. Bushnell, of the mission on the Gaboon River, opposite Corisco. He seemed afraid that our missionary privileges might be restricted at Corisco, as a Jesuit priest was soon to be stationed there by the Spaniards.

"But I had not yet finished giving you an account of my London visit when I closed my last, so I will devote part of this letter to that. After I had visited the British Museum, I concluded to take up my lodgings near the central part of the city. I found a boarding-house right by Charing Cross, which is the great omnibus centre, from which you can get an omnibus to any part of the city. I had very nice quarters. Next morning, going down to the Thames, I took a boat up past the London Bridge to the old Tower of London, so famous in English history. Paying a shilling at the entrance, I found a guide who led the way across the old moat, now dry, into the frowning and massive walls of stone to the Horse Armory.

Here were mock men on mock horses, clad in steel armor which had been worn by kings and nobles from Edward I. (1272) down to James II. (1685). The suits on men and horses were polished bright and clean—beautiful relics of the times that are past. Some of them were of immense weight; a wonderful burden for a horse to bear must have been old Henry VIII., with his own ponderous body and his full suit of steel plate and the armor for his horse! There were armors that a score of other kings (as Henry VII. and Richard III.) and noblemen had worn, and some of smaller size, which had been the property of young princes. In addition to these, there were lances and spears of every age, and swords and pistols and guns innumerable.

"In another room I saw the block on which three Scotch lords had been beheaded, and the head-axe with which Lady Jane Grey was said to have been executed. In another apartment the guide pointed out the *crown jewels*, kept in a glass case surrounded by an iron railing. Victoria's crown was there, resplendent with gold and jewels, also the crown of the Prince of Wales and the queen's golden sceptre, and much other gold and jewels, in value about three millions of dollars.

In another apartment I saw where the prisoners have been kept in ages long gone by. The stones were carved with various names and devices by those who had been confined. In the outer yard was marked the spot where the executions had taken place by the block and axe.

"From the Tower a boatman rowed me to the Thames Tunnel, a remarkable arched road running under the river from one shore to the other. On each side of the tunnel are little shops and stalls for shops — many of them unoccupied — running the whole way. Musicians at different places are constantly making the tunnel ring with their strains, hoping to pick up an occasional penny from the passers-by in return for their melody. While the tunnel was being built, I was told that the water of the river once broke through, and even carried a flatboat through with it. The current was checked by throwing in sand-bags from above. Another curiosity which I saw, but did not travel on, is an *underground* railroad running for several miles immediately under the streets of the city. There are dépôts through the city, and steps leading down to the railroad.

"The last day I spent in the city was chiefly at the Zoological Gardens in Regent's Park, and a delightful place they are to visit. Among all the interesting things that I saw, this was by no means the least. This is a large enclosure, with houses and stalls and large cages, in which are collected all manner of beasts and birds from almost every part of the world. A sixpence was the price of admission. The boys would think it a wonderful treat. The monkey-cage generally had a crowd about it, for the pranks of the creatures were amusing beyond description. Parrots, too, were there from every clime, and bears and lions; an old elephant and a baby elephant; immense hippopotami and giraffes and ostriches—one a most beautiful specimen, with glossy black plumage over him, except the wings and tail, which were white; and for size he was monstrous. As I stood by the enclosure, he reached his head over high above my own. Everything looked plump and in fine condition, very different, indeed, from those that are usually seen in traveling menageries. These immense gardens, with their rare inhabitants, are kept up partly at the expense of the city and partly by private enterprise.

"In the morning of the Sabbath that I spent in London I went to hear the great Spurgeon, as simple, plain a gospel preacher as I ever listened to. His sermons are food for the soul. His tabernacle, which holds five or six thousand, was full, as indeed is always the case, and at nights it is often so crowded that hundreds cannot find seats. It is built with two rows of galleries running all the way round, and his pulpit projects a considerable distance toward the centre. Mr. Spurgeon is a heavy-set man, not very tall, with a round, happy face. He speaks with a clear and distinct voice, but not very loud; no one, I think, however, even the farthest off, has any difficulty in hearing him. He speaks without notes, has but few gestures, and is entirely free from affectation. I went in the afternoon to Dr. Hamilton's church, but found it closed.

"With much love and a happy *new year* to you all, I bid you good-night. And may our Father still bless and protect us, though absent far one from another."

Another letter to his parents from Glasgow is dated

"GLASGOW, Jan. 11, 1864.

"To-morrow, Mr. Thompson (the missionary), his sister, and a Miss Stuart and I, start on a visit to Edinburgh, Melrose Abbey and Abbotsford. This little trip I have been putting off for some time, knowing that I have several weeks for sight-seeing. A long delay it has been, and it might have been a most tiresome one had not the Lord placed me in the hands of such kind friends, who make it their study to show me every possible kindness and try to keep me from thinking the time long; so that, although I have felt anxious to be away as soon as possible and at my work, I have had a most delightful stay in Scotland. I hope I am learning this lesson: to be content with whatever the Lord sends me. I have now some prospect of getting away. The ship Elgiva has not yet arrived, but is reported on the coast of Ireland, and will be in Glasgow perhaps to-morrow. I may expect to sail for Africa about the first of February. I have been waiting so long that now the certain prospect of getting off, though somewhat distant, seems most gratifying. My time has been passed pleasantly enough, but if I could have had my own choice I would have spent more of it in reading and writing. But the family have always had some plan on foot to fill up the time—one day away through the Cathedral and the Necropolis—the cemetery of Glasgow—the last very different from ours. It is a large terraced hill, and every terrace filled with monuments of stone, granite or marble. These are short and thick, so that every terrace gives you the impression of a rampart or fortification of some kind. The hill presents a very grand appearance as it rises in the distance, with its weight of monumental stones and its solemn aspect. There is a fine monument here to the memory of John Knox, though his body lies elsewhere. I saw the grave of Motherwell, the poet. Near by is an inscription to the memory of nine men who were martyred during the persecution in Scotland many hundred years ago. The lines on the stone are peculiar. The last two, speaking of the persecutors, run about thus:

> 'They shall know at the judgment-day
> That to murder saints was no fine play.'

"I went over the Clyde on yesterday (Sabbath) a week, and preached for Rev. Mr. Birkmyer of the Free Church. He is a young man, lately settled in a most important charge. I feel a sympathy for him, for his work will be heavy enough. On yesterday morning I went to hear Dr. Caird, but was disappointed, as he did not preach. The church in which I sat is one in which Dr. Chalmers was for a long time settled (Tron Church), and in which he delivered his great astronomical discourses. In the afternoon I preached for the Rev. Mr. Middleton in one of the oldest churches in the city, which has about twelve hundred members. I preached to as attentive an audience as I ever saw. This I notice among the Scotch—that they give good heed to every one that addresses them. When the minister reads they have their Bibles and follow him. Their singing is altogether congregational. A precentor leads and the congregation all join. I have not seen a church with an organ, and they sing David's psalms, the old version.

"We went to-day to the City Hall to attend a meeting of the National Bible Society, saw quite a large crowd and heard several very good speeches. The Duke of Argyle presided, and made a good speech. A noble man he seems to be, and thoroughly interested in everything good. I heard a speech from the Earl of Dalhousie, and part of one from Rev. Sir Henry Moncrief; so that for one day I saw a good many representatives of the nobility, and worthy specimens they are. There is a most astonishing deference and respect shown to rank here by every one.

"My New Year was spent here. Mr. Thompson's brother and family were all with us. We had a great dinner, like that on Christmas. On Saturday Mr. Thompson and I took a trip into the country and a ramble over the hills at the foot of the High-lands. We met some marks which the old Romans had left when they held possession here—one old stone bridge, in particular, which was built seventeen hundred years ago, in the time of Hadrian. As I go early in the morning I will have to close, for it is now late. This seems to me a very unsatisfactory letter to send so far, but I hope to do better soon, after my return from Edinburgh. Much love to all my friends, and tell them all to write, for I shall be greedy of letters. Good-night, and much love and many blessings on you all."

To his sister he writes:

"GLASGOW, Jan. 27, 1864.

"The *Elgiva* is now on the *slip* being examined, and will likely be off and loaded by the last of this week or the early part of next. Although the delay has been very long, it may all be for the best, for even if we had got off several weeks sooner, like many other vessels, we might still have been tossing about in the English Channel, unable, on account of the winds, to make the open sea. My acquaintance here, too, has been extending, so as to make my stay as pleasant as it could possibly be under the circumstances. I have found a good many Scotch friends, whom I shall always remember with great pleasure, especially the Thompsons, with whom I am staying, who have proved themselves friends such as are worth having. I hope I may never forget their kindness, and never lose an opportunity of showing them that I fully appreciate it all.

"Mr. George Thompson and I started on a trip to Loch Lomond. The weather was foggy and sometimes raining, but occasionally we got a peep at the sun. We took the train down the Clyde to Hellensburgh, and thence struck for the Highlands on foot. The roads were delightful—all macadamized and kept in fine repair. Our way lay right up over the hills, and through the *moors* and *peat beds*, where they get peat for burning; all the landscape around looked splendid, just from its rugged dreariness; all the ground covered with the brown heather, which in the distance looked like whortleberry bushes. We saw a great many heath-fowls, about the size of a pheasant, but no one is at liberty to shoot them without license. We caught a glimpse of some beautiful pheasants on the estate of Sir James Colquhoun—pheasants not such as ours, but with very long tails, and beautiful bright plumage about the neck and breast, originally from China or Persia. On the way we were caught in a driving shower, but took shelter behind a stone bridge. After a walk of about nine miles we came to Luss, stopped at the inn and got some refreshment, and then trudged on three and a half miles farther to Inverngle's inn, on the shore of the lake, and right under the shadow of old Ben Lomond. There we stopped for the night, and had a good supper of ham and eggs. We were none the worse for the walk, except that I had blistered my heel. However, after we got rested and the moon was fairly up, I took off my shoes and put on the landlord's *big brogans*, and away we started for a walk up the lake by moonlight.

"We were now about the centre of the lake (or loch, as it is called, about thirty miles long and from three to five wide), and right opposite stood Ben Lomond, with its top white with snow and covered with clouds. Along the side on which we walked the bare hills ran up almost as high, and the tops were also covered with snow. As we walked along their base, down came rivulet after rivulet, jumping from rock to rock. The music of one had not died away on our ears until we heard the murmur of another. The whole scene was wild, picturesque and beautiful. Its wildness and

strangeness made it seem almost enchanting. After
a while we wended our way back to the inn, feeling in good trim for a sound sleep after about
fourteen miles of a walk.

" Next morning, after breakfast, we climbed up
the mountain side opposite Ben Lomond, and had
a noble view up and down the lake; and while we
stood there, with our heads almost in the clouds, a
wild snow storm swept about us, and far above us
the tops of the mountains were white with snow,
and away through the storm, down on the lake below, we saw the sunshine glistening on the waters;
and along the lake we had seen some roses and
daisies in bloom. In a little nest among these
mountain tops we came across a beautiful little
lake, called the *Fairy Lake*, and from it a good
large stream goes tumbling down the mountain-
side. The Scotch have an old legend connected
with this little lake. The fairies here, in their
mountains, it is said, once had their abode, and at
this little lake they did their *dyeing*, not only for
themselves but for all the people around. As the
fairies were invisible, of course each old lady must
bring her fleece of wool and lay it down beside
the lake, with a piece of yarn thread of whatever
color she wished her parcel to be dyed. But a

certain *wag* at one time brought a *black sheep's* fleece with a white thread on top of it. This piece of malicious waggery so offended and disgusted the fairies that they deserted their beautiful lake, and left the old ladies thereafter to do their own dyeing.

"From this we went down again to the side of the lake, and up along it on a splendid macadamized road until we came to a Mr. M'Farland's, where we took dinner. He had belonged to the old M'Farland clan of Highlanders. Mr. Thompson knew him, having spent some weeks there in the summer. After dinner we went on up to Tarbet, near the other end of the lake, where is a fine large hotel, and some beautiful summer residences, for the accommodation of those who wish to spend their summers on the shore of the loch. Nearly all the land on one side of the loch is owned by Sir James Colquhoun, and he has his residence on a beautiful little neck of land that puts out into the loch. At Tarbet we took the little steamer that plies up and down the lake, and sailed down to the river Swan, which is the outlet of Loch Lomond. Here we took the cars to Bowling, and walked thence to Dun Lochen, where I was to preach for Mr. Slack on the next day. This was one of the most delightful trips I ever had. Dun Lochen is a town of cotton mills, nine or ten miles from Glasgow. The property, amounting in value to perhaps two and a half millions of dollars, was all made and owned by one man; but now he is dead, and the heirs are quarreling over his will.

"On Tuesday I came into Glasgow, and in the evening we had a very pleasant little party.

"*Wednesday*, Feb. 3.—This is my birthday, which completes my 27th year. I hope I may grow in all that is good as fast as I do in years. I was out to take tea this evening at Mr. M'Cormick's. Their son is going out with me as a clerk to the Gaboon River. I felt for the poor mother. As we spoke of his going away, the silent tear would trickle down her cheek, showing the feelings at work within. There are three young men going out on the Elgiva, the only passengers beside myself. They go out as clerks along the coast of Africa. I hope I may be enabled to do them some good on the voyage.

"*Thursday*, 4th.—It seems we are to get off, at last, on day after to-morrow. I am heartily glad of it. To-day I must make some calls, and to-morrow pack up my trunks and send them on board. I will finish my letter to-day, and perhaps put a scrap in to-morrow morning, as it must be mailed to-morrow to get off this week. It will be a long time before you hear from me again, possibly not till the middle or last of June, as it will take about two months to reach Africa, and two months for a letter to return. But do not feel the least uneasiness or anxiety about me. I have firm faith that our God who guides the storm will bring me safely to my journey's end; and even if he should not, still all will be well, for we shall meet again. Let me be often remembered in your prayers, as I know I am, and particularly that I may be a blessing to these young men who go out with me. I long greatly to hear from you all, but I must wait patiently till I arrive at Co-risco. Mr. Thompson and I gathered some mosses and ferns on the banks of Loch Lomond, and Miss Jessie Thompson has arranged them nicely for me to send to you as a memento of my trip.

"And now I pray that the graces of Christ may dwell in us all richly while we live, and that we may all at last sit down together on high.

"*Friday Morning.*—We expect to go down to the bark to-morrow, and perhaps sail out in the night or next morning. I was calling on some of my friends yesterday to say good-bye. I have friends in Scotland whom I will always remember with pleasure. I have my trunks packed, and expect to send them aboard this evening. Good-bye."

To his parents he writes after sailing:

"OUT AT SEA, Feb., 1864.

"I intend to jot down such things as I think may be of any interest to you, as we sail along, and send the result to you at the first opportunity. I wrote you a very short note just as we were putting out to sea, and sent it back by the captain's wife, who came out as far as the tug and went back with it, but I had not time to speak of my departure from Glasgow. On the Saturday evening before I left, we were all out at Mr. George Thompson's brother's for tea—quite a company of us. We had a season of prayer together, and then Mr. George Thompson and I started for Greenock, where we spent the Sabbath. I feel under never-ending obligations to the Thompson family; they have been kind, *very kind* friends of mine, and I hold them in high esteem. If I have ever an opportunity, I will try to show them that I do really appreciate all their deeds of kindness. When I started, they put up for me half a dozen bottles of raspberry vinegar to mix with the water at sea, also two nice jars of jelly and a fine big Scotch cake with fruit mixed in it. They seemed sorry to have me go away, and I am sure that I shall look back with longing many a time for the return of as pleasant hours as I spent in that family. One thing that made my stay delightful and profitable was the high tone of piety and Christian feeling among them all.

" *Tuesday*, 9th.—The tug left us, we put the captain's wife aboard of her, and the sailors started her off with cheers. The captain's little son is along with us, and a nice little fellow he is, but very delicate. His father takes him in hopes that the voyage will make him strong. On the north coast of Ireland, to-day, we passed the Giant's Causeway, which the boys will know about from their geography. The weather is fair, and we were on deck part of the time, but in the afternoon the motion of the ship made us all sick, and we were obliged to roll into bed.

" *Friday*, 12th.—I have not done anything since Tuesday but lie in bed sick, sick—not dangerously ill, but then the most dreadful nausea and vomiting. I was not much troubled with it coming over from New York, but this time I have caught it in its full force. All of us who are passengers are in the same condition. We have a Dutch steward, a very clever old fellow, who watches over us very tenderly, tucks the clothes in about us in bed, brings food, and insists on our eating. This afternoon two or three of us climbed up on deck, and found it quite pleasant, as the sun was shining, but the breeze was pretty cold; we got down, however, behind the boats, and John (Yahn) brought us some boiled potatoes and salt and cold beef, and we made out to eat a little.

" We expect to have morning and evening prayers in the cabin, and preaching regularly on the Sabbath.

" *Tuesday*, 16th.—For the last few days we have been sailing under difficulties. On last Friday night, when we had reached about the 53d parallel of latitude, off the west coast of Ireland, a terrible gale struck us and threatened to blow us away backward. But immediately all hands were on deck, and the sails closely furled and the ship left to drift. So for two or three days we were tossed about at the mercy of the wind and the waves, slowly drifting backwards with the current. Sometimes a great wave would strike us, and make the ship quiver, and again the waves would break clear over us, and send the salt sea in upon us at every crevice, until the floor of the cabin and state-rooms was entirely wet, and also most of the bedclothes. Mine, however, remained pretty comfortable all the time.

The poor seamen had a terrible time of it, as many of them had to be on deck in the midst of the rain and storm. The deck is just a plain flat top, rather narrow, and without a bit of railing. How the men stood up on it in the midst of a gale, while the ship was tossing like an egg-shell, and turning almost halfway over on her side, I suppose only a seaman can tell. Most of us spent rather sleepless nights. Indeed to me it was a time of anxious watchfulness, and much of the time was spent in examining my own heart, to know how my case stood. We were doubtless in a good deal of danger, and it was at least a time when, if ever, one should be thoughtful and anxious to know his case. I endeavored to put all my concerns in the hands of Christ, and to feel that they rested securely there. And yet, oh how I felt that if ever such a sinner as I be saved, it must be 'just so as by fire,' fleeing as a man flees from a burning building, escaping naked from the flames! God knows just how to deal with his people, and I trust he is saying to me in this, 'Fix your eye more steadily on Christ, and never, never remove it until you arrive in glory.'

"On Monday the captain concluded to put back to harbor and wait for a change of wind, and arrange his deck load of boards better; for the boards had been tossed in such a way that it was almost impossible for the sailors to get about over them. He intended to take Belfast as the nearest and best harbor (on the north-east coast of Ireland), but when he got around there this morning, he found such a fine and favorable wind blowing, and everything so promising, that he determined to keep on down St. George's Channel, and out to sea by that way, not stopping at all, but arranging the boards as we go. So here we go to-day down the channel with a fine breeze and the sea as smooth as a lake and the sun out beautifully. We are all over our sea-sickness, and now the sailing is pleasant.

"*Thursday*, Feb. 18.—Last evening we sailed down past Dublin, but too far off to see it. The bay is beautiful, and we saw the hills round about. As we go down the channel we see sails in every direction, and old Ireland in the distance still keeps in view. To-day we are beginning to get things put to rights—bed-rooms cleaned up—and things

wear a more cheerful aspect. The breezes bear us
down the channel at about four or five miles an
hour. The sea is smooth, with scarcely a ripple,
and the sun is out brightly and the day is almost
as pleasant as spring. I spend most of my time
now in reading. I have got hold of a volume
of Rev. E. Erskine's sermons, which are rich
and full of gospel marrow.

"*Wednesday*, Feb. 24.—I have written nothing
since the 18th, chiefly because we have been tossed
up and down most of the time with squalls. At
one time we had to furl our sails and lie to for
twenty-four hours; yesterday morning, however,
we started on our way again at seven or eight knots
an hour, but still the sea is tossing us furiously.
Sometimes we are thrown from one side of the cabin
to the other. Our soup John, the steward, brings
us in bowls, and, instead of putting them on the
table, we hold them in our hands. Our seats are
two hair-cloth sofas—one at each side of the table
—securely fastened to the floor. John is a good
cook, and when the weather is fair, he gets up
a fine dinner, with plum-pudding for dessert.
But when the ship is tossing we take just what
we can get: potatoes, cold meat and hard crackers—*hard tack*, as our soldiers call it—and, as we

have no cream for our coffee, I drink mine in its purity, without sugar.

" The captain, who is a very pleasant man, about fifty-three years of age, gave me one of his caps and a thick monkey-jacket to wear when I go on deck. He shows me every kindness possible. The three young men (fellow-passengers) are all very gentlemanly young fellows. I preached on Sabbath on 'Christ Jesus came into the world to save sinners.' They were all attentive, and I hope the good seed may take root in some. The captain's little son Bob is a nice boy, very bright and intelligent. I am to teach him a little every day. We started from Scotland with two pigs, two birds and two dogs, but they are all dead except one dog; the other dog fell overboard, and the hard weather killed the rest. The severe gales have emptied some of our water-casks which were lying on deck, and it is likely we will put into Madeira to get a new supply; and of this I shall be heartily glad, for I shall have an opportunity of mailing you a letter, as I do not like the idea of your being in suspense till June. The floor of the cabin and state-rooms is quite wet again, and the deck is all the time covered with water—that is, the deck on a level with our cabin floor. We have another small deck over our heads. We are waiting anxiously for bright weather, to get dried out again, and I suppose at the rate we are sailing now, directly south, we shall soon be in a warmer climate.

"*Thursday*, Feb. 25.—To-day at noon we are about 40° N. lat. and 18° W. long., about opposite the Azore Islands. We are driving almost directly south, with a strong wind, from seven to nine miles an hour. The captain says ' if the wind keeps up we may reach Madeira by Saturday morning.' It would be a treat to get our feet on shore for an hour. There has been a ship in sight all day, sailing just ahead of us. In the morning we could see her topsails, and this afternoon we have gained so much on her that we see nearly the whole ship. The sun is shining a little to-day, and the men have their clothes out on the ropes drying. The wind drove us along furiously last night, and before the moon rose it was quite dark. Little Bob was out on the deck and saw the phosphorus shining in the water, and ran in 'to get the lantern to see the fish,' for he said he saw their *eyes* shining in the water.

"I have been reading an account of the labors of John Williams, missionary to the South Sea Islands, and find it very interesting. I have Moffat's travels in South Africa in the same volume. A great portion of my reading is in the Bible, so that I may be the better furnished for the work whereunto I am called. I count it the highest possible earthly honor to be permitted to go and preach the gospel to the heathen. My only trouble is that I feel myself to be so unworthy and so sinful that I am ashamed to lift up my face and call God my father. I feel sure that it is the Lord that has thus marked out my path in bringing me to the heathen, and I trust that one of the important results in thus separating me from all the dear ones that I love in my own land will be that I shall be brought very near to God, and will be enabled to walk very closely with my Saviour. For this I daily pray and strive. I feel that when all earthly friends are far away, and earthly comforts are few, there is no lasting joy to be found, except I find it at the Saviour's side. Pray for me, that this may be my only resort for comfort or enjoyment so long as I am a pilgrim here.

"*Saturday*, Feb. 27.—To-day has been bright and sunny, and the sunset very, very fine. The sky has had something of that pale bluish tint peculiar to Southern skies. Still the air is uncomfortably fresh, and we are anxiously wishing ourselves some degrees farther south. At noon to-day we were about ninety miles north of Madeira, and expect to see it to-morrow morning. The captain has concluded not to land there, because the water is so deep for anchoring in. He may stop at Tene-riffe, or perhaps not till we reach Africa. We have seen vessels sailing in sight to-day, apparently com-ing from the Straits of Gibraltar — a bark and brig and schooner. The sea is quite calm again. This evening I saw several large porpoises darting through the water.

"To-day I have been reading Moffat's mission-ary life in Africa. Truly, it is noble to endure such privations for the sake of rescuing the heathen from death, and making known to them a Saviour's love. There surely seems to me to be no possible doubt as to what was my duty in reference to the heathen. Ah! would I stay at home trying to urge a few *who know their duty* to enter into life, when millions are dying for lack of the knowledge of Christ, and earnestly beseeching us to send them the word of life? But I dare not say that the sac-rifice of home and friends has cost me no pangs. Keenly, keenly have I felt it, and yet my heart ought to swell with praise that I am called to so high an honor, for will not He that has called me make himself far nearer and dearer than ever home or friends could be? So that I be faithful to Christ in all things, and walk closely with him, I shall have no lack of peace and joy.

"*March* 2.—To-day we saw Teneriffe in the distance. It is about settled that we are to land there, if we can get wind enough and in the right direction to blow us into port (Santa Cruz); if we do, I shall have the pleasure of mailing you a letter. Our reason for landing is on account of water. All that we had in the casks is gone, and when the tank was opened they found that in some way salt water had got in, and it is too brackish to drink. We have been making very little progress for days, as the wind has fallen off. The sea is almost as smooth as glass, and we are creeping along at the rate of two miles an hour. The weather is now most delightful, as we have got beyond the region of storms. I think of you at home, shivering over your fires, while the wind and hail make doleful music without. But here the sun is almost too hot to sit with comfort on deck, unless you get in the shade of a sail. The captain, or 'skipper' or 'sea-dog,' as he calls himself—for he is quite a jolly old fellow—employs his spare hours on deck sewing sails or making pants for himself, or making table-cloths, as he came away without a supply. He treats me with every kindness, and readily acquiesces in any proposition for religious services; and now we have preaching on Sabbath, a blessing at every meal, and prayers every evening. It does my heart good when the old weather-beaten captain and the young men and myself bow together around the altar of prayer. I preached on last Sabbath on 'If any man love not the Lord Jesus Christ, let him be anathema maranatha.' I hope and pray that God will bless the truth to many of them.

"On Sabbath morning we passed the Island of Madeira, lying among the clouds away on the distant horizon. Yesterday we seemed to have fallen in with quite a fleet of ships, as five or six were visible on different sides of us. To-day there are no ships in sight. Yesterday I was unwell, and John brought me a cup of tea with *milk* in it. I suppose he brought his '*old coo*' to life for my especial benefit. On Sabbath last, by some process, he contrived to make us milk for our tea and coffee. But on Monday, when we asked him for more, he said, '*De coo is deat till next Sunday again.*' So I suppose he is only going to give us this precious beverage on Sunday, unless we are sick.

"*Saturday*, March 5.—To-morrow morning we hope to anchor in the harbor of Santa Cruz, the principal town on Teneriffe, one of the Canary Islands. For several days we have been hovering around in sight of the island, but were kept off, partly by unfavorable winds, partly by calms, and for one day and night we had quite a severe squall, which drove us away a considerable distance. This morning when we went on deck the first thing that met our gaze was the lofty peak of Teneriffe (about 13,000 feet high), covered with snow, and looking most beautiful in the morning sun. The whole island seems high, and the outline is rough and rugged. It has a population of 200,000 or more, and is about forty-five or forty-six miles long and about half as wide.

"I am heartily glad at the prospect of getting a letter to you so much sooner than I expected, and glad would I be if some stray letter from home could be put into my hands also. But I have faith to believe that you will all be kept in peace and safety. And I trust that I may have your fervent prayers to strengthen and uphold me for many years to come. It is a lasting comfort to know that, although far away from home and friends and all I love, yet we meet around the same throne

5

of grace; and in your supplications my name, I know, is not forgotten. I am anxious to learn about Aaron's fate, and yet my fears are the worst. Often since I left home have I seemed to meet him and hold converse with him in my dreams, just as we used to do when we were together. Whatever you may have heard in regard to him or Uncle James, let me know when you write. How my heart will leap when the tidings reaches me in Africa that this bloody strife is ended, and peace again smiles on our land! I earnestly pray that we may no more be called to mourn the loss of any of our friends swept away by the tide of battle. Jim and Jode are, I trust, now hard at their studies. I am proud of them, and look forward with high hopes to the time when they will become noble Christian men—ministers, I trust, missionaries, it may be.

"I sincerely hope that pa's health will recover, and that he will yet be spared to us for many years. I almost feel as though I would faint in the labors which I am undertaking without his prayers to uphold me.

"We have a long journey yet before us after we leave Teneriffe, but I have firm faith to believe that God will spare me to preach the gospel among the heathen. You will not have an opportunity to hear from me again till we arrive at Fernando Po. Much love; and may you all be greatly blessed with all spiritual blessings in Christ Jesus, is the prayer of your affectionate son.

"P. S.—*March* 7.—We landed on Sabbath morning. I came on shore in hope of finding church-service to attend. I called on the American consul, Mr. Dabney, and found there was no service. Found Mr. and Mrs. Dabney delightful people. They invited me back for tea and for dinner to-day. They introduced me to Judge Dyer and his wife, from Chicago, Illinois. It has been a great treat to meet all these Americans, and they have treated me like an old friend. Mr. Dabney is of American parents, but has always lived among the Portuguese. Mrs. Dabney is from Massachusetts. The American man-of-war St. Louis sailed into port yesterday morning. I have met all the officers, some of them at dinner to-day. I went on board this morning, by invitation of Captain Preble, to see Lieutenant Stewart of Uniontown, Pa. I found him a very pleasant fellow—spent two or three hours with him. The meeting with him here was quite unexpected, as I supposed he was cruising farther south. Everything here is

Spanish, and very strange to me. The climate is like July."

To his sister:

"Off Teneriffe, Wednesday, March 9, 1864.

"This morning the sharp and rugged hills of Teneriffe are fading away in the distance, and we are again out on the ocean for a voyage of a month or more. We set sail last night about 12 o'clock, having stayed in port one day longer than I expected. I have had a delightful visit on the island, particularly refreshing after my long imprisonment on the ocean ; and the sight of American faces, with the warmth and kindness of American hearts, has made it a visit that I shall not soon forget.

"We sailed slowly into the bay in front of Santa Cruz, on Sabbath morning, and anchored about half a mile from shore. The appearance of the island from that distance was very barren and desolate, there being scarcely any trees on it, and the whole having a rugged appearance—jagged peaks with little valleys between covering the whole surface, and these looking as if they had been burnt with fire. As there was no prospect of having service on board, I went ashore with the captain in hopes of finding service. When we landed on the pier we found ourselves in the midst of mulatto-colored Spaniards, many of whom came about us jabbering their half Spanish, half English, wanting to be our guides, and some would follow us wherever we went. One said to me, 'You American?' 'Yes,' I said, and asked how he knew. He pointed to my *square-toed boots* as the indicator—for no body wears square-toed boots but Americans.

"I went to the house of the American consul, over which the stars and stripes float, as he was the only person I knew of that it was probable could talk English, or give me information where I could find a church, etc. My Spanish guide—for one still stuck to me—led the way through the outer door and opened the second, which led me to the court within. The houses here, all built in the Eastern style, nearly all look alike, both of the rich and of the poor—generally two stories high, built of stone, and plastered outside with white lime. They are square, and the roofs all flat, so that the families can sit on them in the evenings. The court is an open square inside, thirty or forty feet long and as many broad. After going into the court, and up stairs into a gallery or porch which runs all around the house, and from which they pass into the rooms,

I met Mr. Dabney and introduced myself. He took me into the parlor, and I told him what I came for, who I was and where I was going, etc. After talking a few minutes, he said he had left Mrs. Dabney at dinner, and she would like to see me. After speaking to her, he returned and invited me to dinner, where I met a cordial welcome from her and a Mrs. Cogswell, their family governess. As I had been to dinner, I only took a banana by way of dessert. I was greatly pleased with Mrs. Dabney; she is a lovely Christian woman, kind-hearted and pleasant. They have three children, but the two daughters, aged thirteen and fifteen, were away on a visit to some other part of the island.

"After talking a while I left with a promise to come back next day for dinner. Mr. Dabney went with me to the hotel, and introduced me to Judge Dyer and his wife, of Chicago, now on his way from Sierra Leone, West Africa, where he had been acting as judge in the mixed court—a court established by the English and Americans for the protection of the coast against slavers. I found Judge Dyer and his wife very pleasant people. The man-of-war St. Louis sailed into harbor after the Florida, which had sailed out a few days before. I learned from Captain Preble and his son and the surgeon that Andrew Stewart's son, of Uniontown, Pa., was on board this vessel, second in command, and I had an invitation from the captain to come aboard the next day. All this was to me a very unsatisfactory way of spending the Sabbath, as I got no quiet or retirement. In the afternoon I walked out of town a short distance for the sake of being alone.

"Santa Cruz is a peculiar looking place, altogether Spanish; population, five or six thousand; very closely built; streets not wider perhaps than twelve feet. But they have very few wagons or carts or carriages; nearly all their transportation is done by packing on ponies, donkeys and dromedaries. The streets are thick with donkeys with panniers thrown across their backs and a Spaniard sitting on top. For packing stone they have a wooden frame thrown across the back of a dromedary; and on the back of one I have seen four big stones two or three feet long by one foot wide and thick.

" Teneriffe was once famous for grapes and wine, but a disease of some kind has almost rooted out grape culture. Now they cultivate the cochineal very extensively, and vast quantities of potatoes, figs, oranges and bananas. The climate is most delightful; a constant sea breeze keeps it moderately temperate. The people are lazy and dirty, and the town full of beggars. The upper classes, however, are quite fine-looking: nearly all have black hair and eyes and rather dark complexion.

"I went aboard the St. Louis on Monday about 10 o'clock, in one of her boats pulled by eight or ten mariners, and spent two or three hours with Lieutenant Stewart.* I found him a very substantial fellow. I met several other officers, all of whom I liked very much. We dined at Mr. Dabney's, had a fine dinner and a very pleasant time. Lieutenant Squires and Dr. Lewis of the St. Louis were there. On boarding the Elgiva I found that the captain had concluded not to sail for another day. After spending the night on the vessel I went ashore next morning, and met Lieutenant Stewart and several of the other officers, and spent most of the day with them, after calling on Mrs. Dabney to bid her good-bye, and promising to write to her husband from Corisco. I think I never met a more pleasant and gentlemanly set of fellows than the officers of the St. Louis. In the evening we were rowed over together to the St. Louis, where we parted with

* This gallant officer went down on the Oneida, near Japan, in 1871, bravely standing at his post of duty.

a hearty grasp of the hand, declaring that we were glad to have met each other. I took dinner with Lieutenants Squires and Marsh at the hotel, one consisting of eight courses, conducted with great quietness and order. I enjoyed my dinner very much, after being so long accustomed to sea fare, though I did not partake of all the courses, nor very heavily of any. Thus ended my pleasant visit to Teneriffe. It cheered me, and helped me to go forward with good courage. So now I am on the ocean not expecting to see land again till we arrive at Fernando Po.

"*Saturday*, March 12.—We are in the trade winds now, and the breeze is strong and fine. The air is quite cool since we left Teneriffe. We have very little variety on board the vessel—just the same thing one day and again the same the next. Sometimes we meet a vessel, and yesterday we spoke one by signal flags — her name Verbena, from Liverpool to Hong Kong, nineteen days out. We telegraphed our name, where from and whither bound. By signal flags she said our name, Elgiva, was not in her book (vessel a new one), and asked us to spell the name, which was done.

"I spend most of my time reading, sometimes studying at the Benga Grammar which Dr. Lowrie gave me, and teaching the captain's son one hour a day. I have read the missionary labors of John Williams in the South Sea Islands, also of Moffat in South Africa, and the life of Henry Martyn, and other volumes, all with great interest, and I trust with great profit. I have had many days of darkness and inward trial since I came aboard, but now the light seems to be breaking in, and I am able to rest with calm peace and confidence in God more than ever before. I have made the Bible my study, for it is the only fountain at which I can drink the living stream. I keep the large one that cousin Susan Lamb gave me always near, and it is a choice treasure.

"My thoughts have been much disposed to centre about home for a time, but not with any feeling of melancholy, for I have never had a moment's thought that it was my duty to do otherwise than as I have done, and all my desire, I trust, is to do as God would have me do, and to grow in grace and in the assurance of peace with God, and to reach the full and perfect stature of a man in Christ.

"The captain found one of the sailors drunk the other day, and immediately put him in irons, handcuffs, and he behaved so outrageously and talked so terribly that he had to gag him. He found out that this fellow, with some others, had broken into the cargo and drank a barrel of ale in bottles. It was a miserable sight to see this man acting like a brute, cursing and swearing most blasphemously. I stayed in the cabin all the while, for I could neither bear the sight nor the sound.

"*March* 16.—Our latitude, 15° north, and the sun pours down with no little power, though a constant breeze keeps the weather from being oppressive. The thermometer stands at 80° in the shade. We are now south of the Cape Verde Islands—ran between them and the coast of Africa. We could tell our nearness to land yesterday by the color of the water. When we are within soundings, or in the neighborhood of land, it is of a light bluish cast, but when out in deep water its color is very dark. We spoke another ship to-day on her way from Wales to the Philippine Islands. The young men, or the 'lazy spoons,' as the captain calls them, help handle the signal flag. They are very pleasant, and ready to help at anything, but the captain is fond of joking them. They don't like the hard biscuit, and John has been making loaf bread; but the captain tells them that he won't humor the lazy 'quill-drivers' any more; but they do pretty much as they please with the old tar.

"I preached on Sabbath on 'the *danger of procrastination.*' About the time service commenced, the mate came in and said the sailors would not come in. I was much surprised and disappointed, as it is in my heart to do them as much good as possible while I am with them, but I preached to the captain, the young men and mate. Next day I found the reason why the sailors had not come was because the mate (whom they do not like) had, in a surly manner, ordered them in, and then for spite they would not come. The vessel I spoke of is sailing alongside of us, about one hundred and fifty yards off. She is a fine large vessel, clean and nice. The two captains have been having a fine chat, but the distance and noise of the waves prevents them from hearing each other easily. I often look at these young men going with us to risk their health and lives in Africa for the sake of money, and think that if I had no nobler or more sacred motives to take me there, I should be at home among my friends. But then I think, again, if men are so willing to live in Africa for the sake of gold, a Christian ought to blush with shame that would not be willing to live there for the sake of souls. What a joy it would be if we could always live with eternity in view—so near in view as to make us forget the little interests of self and time! I am persuaded that one of the greatest regrets, when we come to die, will be that we were not wholly and unreservedly absorbed, soul and body, in earnest efforts for the advancement of the kingdom of Christ.

"*Friday*, March 18, 1864.—This morning we are sailing fast toward the equator—within 8° of it. The sun is almost directly over us, and pours with warmth upon us, but the constant breeze keeps us comfortable. I have not yet felt it necessary to take off my winter clothing. We have a large awning on deck, and under this it is delightful, cool and comfortable. We are now in the region of flying fish. We yesterday saw hundreds, or, I might say, thousands, rising up and flying before us like birds, as the ship sailed along, and skimming away across the waves like swallows for one or two hundred yards. They have every appearance of a flock of snow-birds or swallows at a little distance. Some two or three flew into the ship and fell down on deck; these Bob appropriated for his breakfast next morning. They are a beautiful fish, from six to ten inches long, slender and delicate, very much like a mountain trout, except the spots. They have two finny wings shaped like a snow bird's, which open and fold up right at the gills. They serve the double purpose of fins and wings. They have also two smaller fins farther back toward the tail. As the presence of flying fish indicates the presence of larger fish, the young men put out a line to drag behind the vessel yesterday. They caught nothing, but some creature which we did not see tore away the hook and bait. We have seen some pretty large turtles floating on the top of the water. Yesterday Bob came running in to call our attention to some young whales which he saw in the distance. I suppose they were porpoises of a large size. I caught a glimpse of the back of one, which appeared to be as large as a big bullock.

" *Monday*, March 21.—This is hot weather, but the breeze keeps one tolerably comfortable beneath the awning on deck. The trade winds have failed us now, and we move slowly, three or four miles an hour, and often less. We have reached the latitude of Liberia, 5°, and long. 16°, and we hope, God willing, to reach Fernando Po in about fifteen days. The sea is almost as smooth as glass, but neither bird, beast nor land is to be seen. The *Scotch laddies* spend their time in reading, joking with the captain and each other. We are all anxious to be at our journey's end. I preached to the men last Sabbath on the parable of the prodigal son. They were very attentive. After service I distributed some little books among them, as I had done before. They seemed glad to get them. To-day I finished Dr. Lowrie's 'Two Years in India,' and on Saturday 'Fox's Book of Martyrs.' What a record of suffering for Christ's sake the last is! Those confessors swell the multitude that walk in white before the throne, having been 'slain for the testimony of Jesus.' The noble army of martyrs praise thee, O God!

" *March* 25.—For several days past our sails have been flapping almost idly round the masts for want of air enough to fill them. The sun pours down so directly over our heads that at noon it makes no shadow, and the thermometer stands at 90°. The sky is most beautiful, with its varied cloud-tints on a ground of most delicate blue. As night comes on the sky clouds up, and we have lightning and thunder and rain, sometimes in torrents. The young men have been busy trying to catch some fish, but have only got one, which the sailors call a bonita. I have never seen one more beautiful; its shape is exquisite and its color a bluish purple. One of the sailors, Bob they call him—and a clever fellow he is—fell down with violent pain in his stomach. He has not been well all the passage, and I fear this will bring him to his end. Poor fellow! how he did moan in agony, and said, 'Ah, men, I am gone.' They took him to his berth and gave him medicine, and applied a mustard plaster, which gave him some relief. I went in and sat down by him, and tried to explain the way of salvation to him, and prayed with him. He thanked me heartily when I left, as did some of the other sailors who were in with him at the time. Poor fellows! I wish they knew the way to Christ. I have tried to preach only Christ to them, as nothing else will be of any consequence.

"I have finished the Life of Brainard, and am reading Flavel on 'Keeping the Heart,' and my Bible and Greek Testament. For nearly a week we have been lying almost still, but yesterday we got a pretty good breeze and are now moving along tolerably well. I check all thoughts of impatience at the length of the voyage by remembering that to bear patiently whatever comes, and perform present duty, is serving the Lord just as much as though I were in Corisco. Part of every evening

I spend reading and praying with the sick sailor. He is nearly well now, and I sincerely hope his sickness will be the means of bringing him to God. I preached on Sabbath on the 'healing of blind Bartimeus.' Some were very attentive. I hope some fruit may be gathered unto life eternal.

"You are all daily in my thoughts and prayers, as I know I am also in yours; and what does it signify though we be separated for a little while in doing the Master's will? It is only for a little while, and then we hope for an eternal reunion. My health so far, since I left home, is as good as it ever was, and perhaps better. I hope the climate of Corisco will just suit me.

"*March* 30.—I took my old hat from my trunk to-day to wear on deck, and the sight of it filled me almost too full with thoughts of home. I trust you are all well, though even four months might make vast changes. In another week two years will be gone since the battle of Shiloh. Many a time have I thought of Aaron, and often dreamed of him, since I left home.

"*April* 1.—I stood on the bow of the vessel for half an hour to-day watching the porpoises. They are about the vessel by the hundred, swimming along with us, sometimes jumping entirely

out of the water, and then swimming with their
back fins sticking up, giving the impression of a
drove of mules with only their ears above water.
Most of them are about six feet long, with dark
skin, without scales, like the catfish. The young
men shot at some of them, but that has no effect
on them, even when the ball hits. The captain
says it is eight hundred and fifty miles yet to
Fernando Po.

"*April* 4.—The first shark that we have seen
followed after us nearly all day Saturday. The
men tried to catch him with a hook baited with pork,
but he was too careful. Two or three pilot fish
were swimming with him, most beautiful little creatures, striped all over with purple bars, such as you
see on the zebra. We are now almost immediately
south of the dominions of the king of Dahomey,
so famous for his inhuman cruelties. Had service
yesterday. As I thought it might be our last on
board, I spoke very plainly to the men on the
'strait gate.' They listened very attentively, and
I hope and pray that some of them may enter in."

In his private journal, under date of April 4,
Mr. Paull writes:

"*April* 4.—Spend the time reading religious
books, and especially the Bible. Preach every

Sabbath plainly and pointedly to the men, but nothing save Christ and him crucified. Have done but little talking since I came on board. Others jest and laugh around me, but my thoughts have been engaged within. For many weeks I have been 'eating the bread of sorrow,' because I have been in darkness and have had no light. All my sweets have been turned into bitterness, and I have walked on the borders of despair. I have been truly in the dark, and neither sun nor moon nor stars have appeared for many days. God grant that this may be the fire that shall consume the dross of sin wholly from me."

On the subject of missions he next writes :

"Some would turn aside from carrying on this glorious work by saying that God will not punish those who live in ignorance without the light of the gospel. But what then must become of God's character? He who is all good established a law which is upright and good. 'The soul that sinneth, it shall die.' Mercy may seek to let the transgressor free, but justice, immutable justice, cannot, must not, else it is no longer justice. Under the government of a just and holy God, death must follow transgression so surely as God is a God of truth, whether there has been *light* or whether there has been *no light;* but then, according to scripture, circumstances may mitigate the *severity* of that punishment for which death is a general term.

"It is cheering to know that in some places, at least, the heathen are earnestly pleading for the bread of life—looking out from their darkness to catch the faintest dawn of the morning. It would do your hearts good to hear one tell, who belonged to a station on the west coast of Africa, how, the moment a vessel came to anchor, they all ran down to the beach with the anxious inquiry, 'Have you brought us a missionary?' If none had come, they turned away with sorrowful hearts. But if some one stepped forth and said that he had come to tell them 'the story of the cross,' how they bore him away in triumph with a joy which knew no bounds.

"We ought to make the world conform to our religion, instead of our religion to the world; for Christ and his religion are paramount to every-thing, and ought to be esteemed by us above and before everything. The world and all its concerns, pursued for their own sakes, are the *vilest dross* in comparison with them. Our religion should be the life, the very heart-blood, of every action and pur-suit. If we ploughed and reaped, bought and sold, for Christ's sake, if the busy crowd that pass the streets were eager most of all to win riches and honor for Christ, what a heaven there would be on earth!

"*Thursday*, April 7.—We have no variety in our scenery here, except the change from sunshine to cloud, and from the smooth sea to one a little ruffled by the breeze. I am glad that the truest happiness on earth does not depend on outward circumstances, but upon the heart. Fix it on God, and then we dwell in peace among gathering storms or burning suns, or in the loneliness of the desert.

"John, who is a great friend of mine, has been getting a large canvas bag made for me to put my mattress and blankets, etc., into, and every few days he puts a quantity of figs into my berth for me to eat; and I also discover in my berth a bottle of preserved cherries, one of apples, one of plums, and one of desiccated milk.

"*Monday*, April 11.—Nine weeks to-day we sailed from the mouth of the Clyde, and now we are one hundred and fifty miles from Fernando Po. This has been a long time to be on the water, and yet not longer than vessels usually are in making the trip. Last night one of the young men caught a bird about the size of a robin.   It lit on one of the yards and went to sleep.   A young shark was swimming about the vessel to-day, but as soon as they threw a line over with a piece of pork on it he swam away.

"I preached yesterday, as I suppose, my last sermon to the men, on the first Psalm.   I think I have never so desired, or striven so thoroughly, to preach the gospel plainly, pointedly and simply, as I have to the men here.   I earnestly hope and pray that there may be some fruit.   They have always been most attentive and respectful to me, though I fear they care but little for the gospel and for their own souls.   One of these, however—Mr. McCormick, a noble fellow—I have noticed since Sabbath week reading his Bible regularly every night.   Last night he seemed anxious to talk, and I got opportunity to converse with him.   He is quite serious and concerned about himself, and I earnestly hope it may end in his sound conversion to God.

"I tried to think of you all yesterday as getting ready and starting to church, but when I think of you at any time I have to run backward six hours on our clock, as our time is about six hours faster than yours, so that when it is noon here you are just about rising.

"*Wednesday*, April 13.—To-night, after a long voyage, we have cast anchor at Fernando Po. Early this morning John waked me up to say that it was in sight. As we sailed on the dim outline became more distinct, and at length we saw the green hills, covered with the most luxuriant growth of green trees and bushes. As we sailed into the bay, a most delightful odor of flowers floated off to greet us. Before we put anchor down a boat came off the island to meet us, in which was Mr. Murray, whom I had met in Scotland. He arrived here before us by the mail steamer. His boat was pulled by four Kroo boys, as they call them, the first native Africans that I have seen.

"*Thursday*, 14th.—This morning we opened our eyes on a beautiful sight. We lay at anchor in a semi-circular bay of great beauty, and the beach all around us rising to the height of perhaps fifty feet above us. On this high beach the little town of St. Isabel is built. Behind the town the ground gradually rises till it terminates in a peak about 10,000 feet in height. The island, so far as we can yet see, seems to be one of exquisite beauty, covered with tropical plants, fruits and flowers. Cocoanuts I see growing in the greatest abundance on the tops of the tall, straight palm trees; oranges, pineapples and mangoes also. The mango is something like an apple, said to be very fine, but not yet ripe. Plantains and yams are here also. Although vegetation is so rank and fruits so abundant, the animal kingdom is but sparsely represented. They have no animals except those brought from other parts of the coast, as a few sheep, goats, and little bullocks about the size of a large sheep. There are perhaps one or two horses on the island, but the climate is such that no animals can be reared.

"The town of St. Isabel, the only one on the island, has about twenty houses; these are occupied by the Spaniards, as they are the owners here. Their buildings are frame, painted white, and covered with thatch, one story high, and open inside up to the roof, so as to look like a barn within. Although there are a good many Spaniards and some Englishmen, there are no white ladies here, except one, a niece of the old ex-Governor Lynslager. I went on shore to-day with the captain, and he introduced me to Mr. Wilson, the agent of Mr. Laughland, and also vice-consul. We went around and took breakfast with him about 10 o'clock; afterwards he took me to call on the ex-Governor and the Spanish judge. I am to stay with Mr. Wilson till I get away to Corisco, which I shall not be able to do for two weeks.

"*Tuesday*, 19th.—On Friday, about 3 o'clock, Mr. Wilson and I started on foot up the mountain, some six miles, to see Consul Burton. The clouds seemed to promise us a heavy shower, and prudence suggested that we take a change of clothes; and thus equipped, each with a long African staff in hand, we set off, followed by four negroes—for negroes are plenty here—one carrying Mr. Wilson's matters, which he always takes with him, another our carpet-bags, another our umbrellas, etc. We passed through the town, which I found to be much larger than I expected, not having seen the most of it before on account of the numerous plantains, cocoanut and orange trees, in the midst of which the houses are built. There are, I judge, several hundred inhabitants in the town, chiefly negroes from other parts of the coast; and some of them have obtained wealth by trading, to the amount of thousands of dollars. The natives of the island are all proverbially low, and live out in the bush. Their houses are as good as any on the island, some of them handsomely furnished, too, even their tables abundantly supplied with silver.

"After passing out of town we found an excellent road, made by the Spanish governor, leading up to Basili, where he and Consul Burton are now staying, and where the Spanish soldiers are quartered on account of their health. It is the only road on the island, and there seems to be no need of any other. The *Boobies* or natives have their paths, by which they travel through the bush. On either side of us we found the vegetation so rank and thick that breaking a path through it seemed an utter impossibility; the deep black soil and the constant alternation of warm sunshine and rain make tropical vegetation almost incredibly rank and luxuriant. The trees grow to an enormous height and size—the cottonwood especially—six or seven feet in diameter. One palm tree I noticed, a beautiful specimen, ran up to the height of ninety-six feet without leaf or branch, and its diameter (about eighteen inches) seemed to be the same at the top as at the bottom. We had constantly our ears filled with the chatter of crickets and insects, and the songs of birds, which we could never see, as they were hid by the dense foliage of the bushes and trees. We saw no wild animals or game of any kind, and there is but little on the island.

"We crossed one creek and several smaller streams of beautiful clear water as they came tumbling down their rocky beds on the mountain-side, reminding me of our own mountain streams at home. About halfway up the mountain we came to a village of *Boobies*. Their huts are almost hid in the bushes, being very low, and only a very small patch cleared around each one. They seem to be merely a pen, made by driving stakes in the ground, and roofing them with a thatch of palm leaves; they are about fifteen feet long by ten wide and seven or eight high. The Spanish priests have built one or two good frame houses at this village, and are living among the natives, attempting to instruct and civilize them. These *Boobies* seem to be a simple-hearted people, but very stupid. They wear no clothing, or, if any, a yard of calico would make it all. Their faces and arms are horribly disfigured by tattooing. We reached the consul's house, or Basili, as it is called, about 5 o'clock. The consul came down the steps to meet us, and gave us a hearty welcome, as he and Mr. Wilson are great friends. As we were quite wet he hurried us off immediately to change our clothes, which we soon did, and came out with a good appetite for dinner after our walk of six miles, and an ascent of perhaps two or three thousand feet.

"The captain is a very gentlemanly man, very intelligent, fluent and outspoken. He remembered Mr. Flenniken * and the boys, Thomas and Henry, and inquired very kindly for them all. He spends his time writing, very busily, and finds he can do much more up in the mountains than down below. The house he lives in is a very nice one, of frame, one story high, set on high posts, as all are on the island. As they have no horses nor mules nor cattle here, all the wood to build it was packed up the mountain by negroes. From the porch we had a fine view of the ocean and the harbor below, and the air was refreshing and delightful; though I really have not felt it hotter here anywhere than in the summer at home. The captain has several negroes up there with him. I saw four little boys, about twelve years of age, which the famous King of Dahomey made a present to him. These, he says, he intends keeping to support him in his old days. After a lunch of tea and pineapple in the morning, we started down the mountain before breakfast, and the captain came with us a mile or two for the walk. His style of dress was rather primitive— a cassimere shirt without a coat, and his pants stuffed into his boots, and a broad-brimmed

* Judge Flenniken, of Pittsburg, Pa.

hat and a long staff completed his attire. We reached the consulate in time for a hearty breakfast, as we usually had breakfast between 9 and 10 o'clock, and took dinner between 5 and 6 o'clock. I went off to the Elgiva in hopes of preaching to the men on Sabbath, but could not get an opportunity. The Spaniards will not allow any Protestant service to be held on the island.

" *Wednesday*, April 20.—I am spending my time most pleasantly at the consulate, where Mr. Wilson lives, and Captain Burton also when down from the mountain. It is a delightful place. The house is large, open inside up to the roof, walls and partitions well painted, and the rafters whitewashed. It stands right on the high beach, overlooking the bay. Behind it is a large garden, in which are cocoanuts, plantains, pineapples, mangoes, etc. I have been treated with the greatest kindness and attention here as everywhere else. Indeed, it often melts me to think how God has raised up friends for me everywhere, who treat me with the greatest kindness and consideration, as though I had been one of their old friends all my life. Nothing is ever lost by being kind to others, and, indeed, I more and more feel that the less we live for self and the more for others the nearer we come to the spirit of Christ. 'He that saveth his life shall lose it,' and he that is willing to wear away his life in kind deeds to others shall save it.

"*Friday*, 22d.—From my back window I see distinctly the Camaroons Mountains on the mainland, towering up to a great height. Captain Burton ascended the highest peaks, and has written a book in which he gives an account of them. Mr. Wilson and I went down to have a sea bath last evening. Sea baths here are most delightful, as the air and water are comfortably warm. Three or four black 'boys' went with us to carry towels, and mats to stand on, and Batanga canoes for us to sail in. These are quite narrow, and the least tilt will turn them over; but they are so light that a man will easily carry one twenty feet long. The boys, used here for everything, are Kroomen brought from the coast. They are good fellows to work, sprightly and intelligent, and generally stay from home a year. The natives do not often come in to town, except to bring their palm oil, which is almost the only product of the island.

" In the way of living here, where ships come so often, we have almost everything that you have in *civilized* life, and the tropical fruits in addition; but the cost is greater—a little chicken, half a dollar; an egg, half a dime; beef, etc., in proportion. Most of it is sent out from England preserved in cans. All the cooking is done by men trained to it, so that the life of a trader here is very much like the life of a planter in the South.

"*Monday*, 25th.—Our beautiful bay seems full of vessels, some of which have come in from different parts of the coast to await the arrival of the mail. We have some visitors on the island—three or four ladies from the Calabar mission, about one hundred miles north, on the mainland. They are all Scotch ladies. I thought to have preaching again on the Elgiva yesterday, but the captain did not find it convenient.

" *Tuesday*, 26th.—Yesterday I had a most pleasant surprise. Mr. Mackey, from Corisco, supposing that I would be here, came up to meet me on a Spanish vessel which had been at Corisco. He says they have been waiting anxiously for me, as they are short of help. One of the most pleasant parts of the surprise was, that he brought my letters that had already arrived at Corisco.

"*April* 28.—This morning our regular monthly mail came in, and brought me letters, so that I have had a great feast in the letter line. In Lizzie's letter of the 15th January, she gives the sad tidings of

Aaron's death. May the God of all grace comfort you all! I will write after I get to Corisco. I am anxious to hear all the particulars about his death. Mr. Mackey is off in the harbor, trying to get us a passage by the French steamer. If he succeeds, we go down this morning. Long ere this reaches you I hope to have entered on my solemn work, I trust with deeper, truer and more solemn views of life than ever I had before. May very many prayers follow me from the family circle! It will be another month before we hear from each other. Let each succeeding month find us more earnest in the inquiry, 'Lord, what wilt thou have me to do?' and in our efforts simply to believe in Christ."

The following letter to an intimate friend, written from Fernando Po, West Africa, April 26, 1864, evinces Mr. Paul's missionary spirit and care of his own Christian life :

"Away across the wide waste, from all the dear ones that I love, I sit to-day where darkness is as the *shadow of death ;* and I would not have it otherwise. Not because I do not love my friends, not because it gives me no pangs to go down into and remain in the dark valley of this separation, but you know that I always felt and prayed that one end in leading me into the wilderness, as it were, might be my purification. And if God carries on his own work thus, in his own way, what are all other things to me in comparison to it? I know I shall be the happiest man on earth if Christ in his fullness dwell in me, though my name should never be breathed beyond the borders of this dark land. I have had many dark hours since I left you ; indeed, for weeks during my voyage, no light, 'neither sun nor stars, appeared ;' the waves and the billows went over me. I could not tear my eyes away from peering into that deep, dark pit of sin within me, although I knew well that no peace or light could come from it, and that Christ only could give me light. But most heartily do I thank my God for these days of darkness ; for you know that beautiful hymn, 'I asked the Lord that I might grow,' etc. That is the way up out of darkness into light. I believe there is no other way ; and now my prayer is, My God, let the darkness come if thou wilt only lead me in it, and bring me forth into entire consecration to Christ.

"I think I have only lately begun to see that in our religion we ought to be most *terribly in earnest*, even storming the kingdom ; for how else can we take it? I hang my head with shame whenever I think how halfway I have been all my life, and how miserably halfway and undecided I always shall be, unless God take my case in hand. Do you not often find yourself forgetting that it is appointed unto us to enter into that strait gate by *striving*, or that we are to gain the crown by coming off conquerors—attacking, sword in hand, the armies of the aliens within us, searching them out diligently, and constantly slaying them one by one, till not any enemy remains to raise his voice against the reign of Christ within us?

"But about Africa I have, as yet, said nothing. Now, by the goodness of God, I have my foot on her heathen soil, and I humbly pray that it may never be removed until I be made instrumental in claiming some of her children for God. Without doubt death reigneth here. The trail of the serpent is deeply marked over all the land. The *shadow* lies so heavily on the land, that the courage and zeal of the strongest must fail if he rests on a human arm. But I am glad and satisfied when I know that He whose word is power has promised that the Son shall have his inheritance here, that Ethiopia shall stretch forth her hands unto God. True, God has not said when this glorious consummation shall be brought about, but we know that the leaven which we put into the meal will work, though we see it not, and the bread (seed) which we cast upon the waters will bear the rich harvest (fruit), though it be after many days.

"Give your little son a hearty kiss for me. I pray that he may be a lamb, carried in the arms of the great Shepherd. Try to get the love of Christ mingled with his very life, so that it may grow with his growth. Why ought we not to hope that the little ones, above all others, should be attracted by the sweetness and loveliness of Christ? If we constantly present Christ to their little loving hearts in all the attractive features of his character, I do not know how it is possible for them to help loving him. They cannot but be melted by displays of love and kindness such as Christ has made; and if we keep these before them, they must sink into the heart and transform the life."

Mr. Paull here uses strong language in recommending religious instruction and example as means of grace to children, yet he was a firm believer in the doctrine of original sin and total depravity, and the absolute necessity of the Holy Spirit's work in regeneration.

To his father he writes whilst voyaging again from Fernando Po to Corisco:

"On Schooner 'Estremadura,' April 29, 1864.

"This evening Mr. Mackey and I bade farewell to Fernando Po, with many pleasant recollections of the kindness received from Mr. Wilson and others. Our next resting-place is on the little schooner which is to take us down to Corisco, a vessel belonging to Mr. Laughland, and running between his trading-points on the coast. Accommodations for traveling here are but meagre, but one feels thankful to get almost any mode of conveyance. Two of the young men that came out with me on the Elgiva are with us, going down to the Gaboon River. We four, with the captain and his wife, filled up the little cabin to overflowing, leaving scarcely any room to move. To relieve the monotony of his voyages the captain keeps on board two parrots and a Scotch terrier dog, and by the kindness of Mr. Wilson a little goat is added to complete the list.

"*May* 1.—This morning we are sailing slowly down the channel between Fernando Po and the mainland. The channel is, I suppose, about forty miles wide. The winds are so light along the coast here that it generally takes a week to make the trip—two hundred miles.

"We had service on deck to-day. As Mr.

Mackey is feeble, I officiated. Spoke to them from the twenty-third Psalm.

"*May* 4.—We have been sailing all the while in sight of the mainland, though five or six miles distant. There are few mountains, but the high hills run all along the coast, rising up behind one another tier after tier. There are no places of interest to be pointed out, no cities, no grand old ruins, but all is one wild wilderness save here and there, at the mouth of some river, you find a little native town. To-day we were amused to see a lone mariner sailing bravely by us—a bird near the size of a pigeon, perched on a cocoanut, or something of that size, riding coolly along and keeping his balance, never heeding the tossings of the waves as at one time they sent him up to the top and again down to the bottom.

" *Friday,* May 6.—This afternoon my long journey is ended, and I stand at last on my island home, with a heart full of gratitude to God that he has preserved me in all my journeyings, and especially that he ever put into my heart to come and preach his gospel to the heathen. The captain anchored two or three miles off shore, and Dr. Nassau came off to meet us with a boat. As our baggage was considerable, one of the schooner's boats had to come off with us and carry part of it. Corisco is a beautiful little gem of an island, covered with verdure of the deepest green. All around it lies a sandy beach, white almost as the snow, over which the huge waves surge and break unceasingly. Mr. Mackey and I were in a boat together, and when we landed went immediately to his house, on a little eminence about one hundred yards back from the beach, and in full view of the sea and in hearing of its unceasing thunder-like roar. Mrs. Mackey gave me a hearty welcome to my new home, and now I feel once more as if I had found a resting-place for the sole of my foot, and could settle down in quietness to my work. You will be glad to know that I am to make my home with Mr. and Mrs. Mackey.

"And now I wish you could look over, for a moment, into Africa, and catch a glimpse of this home of beauty in the heart of heathenism. It would make you glad, as it has gladdened me. It would make you feel as you can fancy some traveler upon the sandy desert would were he to light upon a garden of blooming flowers. So this little home of Mr. Mackey's, 'Evanga-simba,' has been fitted up with such taste that I never would desire anything more beautiful. The house is neat and large, with broad verandas running round it. The grounds are planted with fruit trees and flowers—the orange, lemon and lime, plantain, banana, cocoanut, etc. In the little pasture lots about you see a pony and some cattle, goats and sheep, rabbits, ducks and chickens; so that, in point of comforts such as these, there is no lack. They live here as civilized people do in America or anywhere else. I have a sleeping-room in Mr. Mackey's house up stairs, and a very nice study in a bamboo house in the yard."

In his journal of this date Mr. Paull speaks of the Kroomen:

"There is a tribe of Africans from Cape Palmas, called Kroomen, and known all along the coast. They usually hire themselves out to traders and captains of vessels, often ten or twelve in a batch, under a head man, who becomes responsible for the risk. These Kroomen are mostly stout and well built. They generally hire themselves for a year, and then return home with the proceeds of their labor. Most of this is plundered from them by the older ones, and with what is left they buy a wife.

" Their heads are shaved in all fantastical shapes. Their faces, too, are marked usually with a black streak down the forehead and nose, also an arrow-head at the corner of the eyes. They delight in strings of large beads around the neck and wrists, sometimes cowries and tigers' teeth around the ankle. Hardly any clothes except the loin-cloth and perhaps an old hat or vest.

"They seem to drink water always after their food, and are particularly careful of their teeth, cleansing them always after eating, generally carrying a little wooden brush tied about their necks with a string. They talk broken English, most all smoke their short, black pipes, are fed on rice, and have their long-toothed wooden combs.

" *Monday*, 9th.—Yesterday I went to church. The meetings are held in a large bamboo church near by. Dr. Nassau preached in English and one of the black boys interpreted it to the congregation, which was mostly composed of young people belonging to the mission schools. They are as neat, nice-looking black children as I have ever seen anywhere. We had Sabbath-school in the afternoon. I taught a class of young men, some of whom understood English. At night Mr. Mackey preached or explained the first chapter of Ephesians in English, which was interpreted.

"It did my heart good to feel that I was thus

worshiping God in this land of darkness, and to know that he had at last answered my prayer and brought me as a missionary to Africa. Now, since he has done thus much, my unceasing petition is, that he will consecrate me wholly to him and use me entirely for his glory. It seems to me nothing can be done here without prayer, unceasing prayer. The minds of the heathen are so dark and ignorant and debased that nothing but a ray of heavenly light can penetrate them.

" There are, I think, twelve hundred on the island, which is about three miles long and three wide. The people live in little villages of a dozen houses or less, built near the sea-shore. Their houses are built of bamboo poles split in two, and tied one above another to stakes driven in the ground; the floors are of hard clay. I see no difference between the natives here and the negroes at home, except that here they wear scarcely any clothes. They seem to be as apt to learn and as intelligent looking as any. They nearly all wear a heavy roll of small beads of various colors around their necks, and the women wear brass rings around the ankle, extending one above another sometimes nearly to the knee.

" The old king was in this morning to see us.

He wore an old dingy silk hat and black coat, and a large piece of light muslin wrapped around him extending down to his feet. He carried a butcher-knife in a sheath belted around his waist; so do most of the men. He wished Mr. Mackey to tell me that he settled all the affairs of the black men and his brother of the white men on the island. This was, I suppose, to give me some idea of his position. He is an amiable and quiet old man. They look with great interest and curiosity on a stranger. A great many have been in to see me and shake hands with me. When I am on the veranda I see many of them stopping to look as they pass. I observed one woman with a little child in her arms standing and pointing to me for a long time, trying to get the child to look at the stranger.

"There are three stations belonging to the mission on the island, one here (Evangasimba), and Ugobi and Alongo at different points. There are two excellent houses here (at Evangasimba), one occupied by Mr. Mackey and the other by Dr. Nassau and Mrs. M'Queen. Ugobi and Alongo are occupied by native teachers while Mr. Clark and Mr. de Heer are away. Mr. Mackey has a carpenter shop, and native carpenters, who have

Evangasimba Station.

p. 106.

been trained, making boxes, which are exchanged for goods to the traders. He has a store-house also, in which he keeps goods to buy food from the natives, and pay them for work, etc. Everything needed is sent out by the Board with vessels coming to Gaboon River, so that there is nothing to prevent our living comfortably. We have good coffee and tea and sugar, and sometimes goat's milk for cream, also excellent bread and sweet potatoes and goat's flesh, and fish and roasted plantains and tomatoes, rice, eggs, bananas and oranges, etc. There is plenty of corn on the island, so that we can have roasting-ears and mush and corn bread. So you will not, I hope, feel any anxiety about my personal comforts. I am as happy and contented, and am as well cared for, as I could be anywhere in the wide world except at home. Never for an hour since I left have I doubted that I was in the path of duty, nor ever have I been happier in my life than I am now in the contemplation of this, I trust, my life-work among the heathen. The climate here is delightful. The sun is hot, but it is easy to carry an umbrella. The nights are cool enough to sleep under a blanket. With the blessing of God, I see nothing to prevent me from enjoying good health. As this is the wet season, we have rains almost every day, but the soil is sandy and the water is soon absorbed.

"*Thursday*, May 12.—To-day we had a meeting of the mission to consult as to what course I should pursue. They suggested that I go to the study of the language. Mr. Mackey has secured an interpreter (Ubengi) for me at twenty cents a day. He is to come to-morrow, and I commence work in earnest. I have been trying to pick up a few words, and have about thirty. I am anxious to learn the language as soon as possible, so as to preach in it.

"Mr. and Mrs. Mackey and I went up this evening after tea to the girls' school, kept by Dr. Nassau and Mrs. M'Queen. The Doctor invited us up to hear the children sing. They have about fifteen little girls, between the ages of seven and twelve or thirteen. They were all neatly clad, and as intelligent, nice-looking black children as I ever saw in America. You would never know them to be heathen if you saw them in a Christian land. Dr. Nassau led them, and they sang quite a number of hymns, both in Benga and in English. I surely never heard sweeter singing. I thought, those of them who are saved will sing no less sweetly in heaven for having been born in a heathen land. They learn very fast. Most of them will commit a hymn by having it read over to them a few times line by line. This seems to be the truest and surest way of carrying on the work in Africa, by commencing with the children; though even some of them, after having been trained up and made a profession of religion, are led astray into sin by the heathenish practices of those around them. Nearly all the little girls in the school are already *betrothed*, and will marry at about the age of fifteen or sixteen. A wife costs about one hundred dollars here, and they are very difficult to be got at that, for this reason, they are betrothed so young. Almost the greatest difficulty the missionaries have to contend against is polygamy. A man is usually looked down upon with contempt that has but one wife; some have fifteen or twenty. It is said that yesterday one of the chief men on the island had three people killed because they were supposed to have bewitched one of his relatives who died a short time ago. This is yet the habitation of horrible cruelty.

"*Saturday*, May 14.—Yesterday Ubengi came, and I made a commencement in the Benga. I have him with me from 8 o'clock till 11 o'clock.

He is quite an intelligent fellow, and understands English pretty well. As there is no complete grammar in the language, nor any lexicon, I have to proceed by learning the words and the structure of the language from hearing him talk, and having him read out of the Benga Testament. If I am allowed to go on uninterruptedly with the study of the language, I hope to be able to preach in it in less than a year. But if I find it necessary to take charge of a station, preach, etc., as is likely—for Mr. Mackey has about decided to leave for England in ten days—it may take me two years, or even three.

" I see several varieties of very pretty birds flying around, mostly small ones, and some of them beautiful singers ; and parrots in any number I see flying around over head. They are only visitors, having their homes on the mainland. I have not been around over the island much yet, as it is covered with a thick growth of underbrush, and there are only narrow footpaths running through it here and there. The little gray pony (Mr. Mackey's), about as large as a yearling colt, is now in my charge, and I shall, perhaps, make a tour round the beach on him some day.

" *Monday*, May 16.—Heard Mr. Mackey preach

yesterday to the natives. He makes the services very short, as the natives soon become weary. I taught a class in Sabbath-school, and at night preached in English, and without an interpreter, as most of those present (adults) were able to understand English. To-day we had a meeting of the mission to let Mr. Mackey get away to England for his health. It seems a sore blow to the mission, so weak before, and now the work to be done almost overwhelming to those who remain. But our help is in God: 'when we are weak then are we strong.' He may be just bringing us to our knees so that He may undertake for us. Besides the work on the island, there are stations on the mainland that must be visited and looked after. Dr. Nassau and I have divided the work between us. He will preach here, and I at Alongo and Ugobi. The business part of it we also divided, as that part has grown to considerable dimensions. They appointed me treasurer of the mission. There is about three thousand dollars' worth of goods on hand for the supply of the mission schools, to exchange for labor, food, etc. This comes under my department, so that if I had a good knowledge of business I could use it here."

[It must be remembered by the reader that ordinarily trade is carried on at Corisco by barter, not by money; hence the necessity of goods with which to pay for labor or purchase supplies.]

"*Sunday*, May 22.—It seems not an inappropriate use of this Sabbath evening to write you a few last words before my letters go, as Mr. Mackey takes them with him when he sails, to-morrow morning at 2 o'clock, for Fernando Po, to take the steamer for England. We have had a delightful day of Sabbath privileges in this African darkness. Mr. Mackey preached this morning to a full house of heathen, who had gathered in because of his going away. In the evening Dr. Nassau preached, and we had one or two prayers after service, and an address from Mr. Bushnell of the Gaboon mission, who came over yesterday to bid Mr. Mackey good-bye.

"My health, I am thankful to say, is very good, perhaps never has been better. My sea voyage seemed to have so good an effect on me, that when it ended I weighed one hundred and sixty-four pounds—more than ever I have known myself to weigh. I often think of you all, and greatly desire you to remember me continually in your prayers. Greatly do I long for entire devotion to God, and for the removal of everything in me which hinders the constant indwelling of the Holy Spirit. I am happy and perfectly contented in the prospect of the work before me, and have no unhappiness or sorrow except because of the sin that is in me."

To his parents:

"Corisco Island, W. Africa, May 24, 1864.

" Yesterday morning I accompanied Mr. Mackey to the beach to see him off for England. We all hope he may be granted a speedy return, for we scarcely know how to spare one from our small force.

" My new business of treasurer commenced on Monday, which is the day for paying off the employed with goods, and the natives who are not in any way employed by the mission, many of them, come to buy, and cannot see why they should not be accommodated. They bring money, while they have it, obtained from the Spaniards who are building on the island. Mr. Bushnell went off this (Tuesday) morning to Gaboon in his little sail boat, about as large as a skiff; you would think it too frail a boat to navigate the seas. I went to the beach and saw him off. He is a warm-hearted, Christian man, who keeps his ' lamp trimmed and burning.'

" I had not been to see either of the other

stations (Alongo or Ugobi) on the island; but to-day Dr. Nassau and I went over to Alongo, on the north corner of the island, three miles away. I rode the pony, but found it tiresome, as my feet reached almost to his hoofs. We traveled along the almost snow-white sandy beach, a broad and beautiful place to ride. All along lay sea-shells and coral and stranded seaweed, and the white surf with a continual roar broke on the beach and rolled almost to our feet. Alongo is Mr. Clemens' place, and after him Mr. Clark's, but in his absence a native teacher (Ibia) has charge of the school. It is a most beautiful place, on the highest point of the island, and with a full, broad view of the sea. This is to be my preaching place, and I made arrangements to commence next Sabbath. A good many of the people were met along the shore; some of them had their nets spread out drying. These, I believe, are made of cocoanut fibre, and are used for catching turtles, of which there are many and large ones. They give us, as we pass, their salutation, which is 'Bolo,' or if they are saluting two or more, 'Bolani.' The reply you are expected to make is, 'Ai Bolo' or 'Bolani.' This takes the place of our 'How do you do?'

"*May* 25.—To-day I have not done anything

at the 'Benga,' as I have been somewhat feverish since last night; and when signs of fever show themselves here all study must be laid aside, lest it increase the fever. Two of the Spanish priests were over to-day from where they are building their house, to borrow tools and buy some things from the store-house. I was perplexed to understand them, and to get them to understand me. We are on good terms with them, and think it better, by all means, to live peaceably with them, if possible; but it is not likely that they will let the peace continue after they are once settled.

"I have not yet given you an account of our mode of living here, which I must do that you may have a better idea of mission life. We rise a little after daylight, and before the front door is open there will be perhaps half a dozen people about it with something to sell—eggs or cassada (which is a root of the nature of a yam or potato, and the children of the mission school are fed on it)—or perhaps they want to buy something, or maybe only want to sit a few minutes to look or talk. At half-past six the bell (which hangs at the side of the house) rings for prayers, and all about the premises are expected to come in. Mrs. Mackey then hears the girls recite a verse each in Benga, and then we have prayers and breakfast. At 8 o'clock the bell rings again and all go to work, the carpenters in the shop and two men to cutting weeds about the mission grounds, the girls to their books, and I with my interpreter to the study of the language till 11 o'clock. At 12 o'clock every one quits work and we have dinner. I generally spend the afternoon in reading, writing and studying, and hearing the boys recite English. The bell rings at 2 o'clock for the men to go to work, and at 5 o'clock for them to quit, when we have supper. The men have thus much spare time to get their own food, which is generally a little fish and cassada. I try to go to bed here between 9 and 10 o'clock, for if we lived here with the same recklessness as in America life would soon go. The people come to trouble me through the day to get things from the store-house, but as it breaks up one's time to no purpose, Mrs. Mackey tells them to go away and come back in the evening or early in the morning.

"*May* 31.—For several days my pen has been at rest, and I myself for most of the time laid on the lounge, with my first attack of African fever. I had only a slight attack, which lasted about three or four days, but did not confine me to my bed. Utter prostration and pain in the back, with headache, were the most uncomfortable features about it But with the plentiful use of quinine and other medicines, coupled with two visits a day from Dr. Nassau, I got over it in time to preach on Sabbath at Alongo.

"I had a pleasant ride to Alongo on Sabbath morning, except that the tide was in so far as to be constantly dashing about the pony's feet and wetting mine. I met several natives on the beach, about one-third of the way up, and as I knew them I asked them to come along to church. They said, 'Is this Sunday?' I said, 'Yes.' They replied, 'It is too far to go to Alongo; we go to Evangasimba.' I said, 'Well, go to Evangasimba.' But one boy did trot after me to Alongo, and called out to the people as we passed through the little native towns, in language which I did not understand, but suppose meant, 'Come to church;' at any rate, a good many of them came.

"I had a very good congregation, composed of the boys in school (I preached in the school-room) and a good many natives. They were very attentive, more so than I expected, for you generally see them dropping off to sleep or yawning, or talking or going out. Ibia, one of the native teachers, who has charge of the Alongo school, was my interpreter. I found that I could speak with almost as much freedom and warmth as when I preach without the interruption of interpreting. I had to make my sermon quite short, as they soon grow weary. I preached on 'Christ Jesus came into the world to save sinners.'

"When I started away on my pony most of my congregation (those who came up from the towns) came trotting after, laughing and hallooing to see the pony carrying a man. About a dozen of them followed me about a mile, just out of friendly curiosity and to get a good laugh. Sometimes, in a narrow place, and to keep from being caught by the tide, I had to put the pony to the gallop, but as I galloped they ran and kept up. At last they all went back.

"When Mr. Clemens first commenced preaching at Alongo, he would tell those that he met on the beach that it was Sunday, and they must come to church, and not fish, etc. So, after that, they were afraid to let him see them fish on Sunday; and when they did venture to do it (the women do all the fishing) a part would fish while the rest watched for him, and if they saw him coming they would scamper off, crying 'Sunday is coming! Sunday is coming!' Heathen soil is hard to cultivate, but He

to whom belongs the seed will make it grow sooner
or later, and I will sow in hope, and perhaps,
sooner than we anticipate, the harvest will come.

"I went down to Peter's town to-day, in hopes
I had enough words to talk a little Benga to him;
but I made poor work of it. Peter is one of the
head men, a kind of patriarch or head of a family,
which he has gathered about him in a little town.
His wives, three or four perhaps, and slaves and
children and younger brothers make up a town of
perhaps twenty houses; only one room in them, of
course. They are set about an equal number on
each side of a street which is, I think, fifty yards
long, occupying about half an acre, and beyond
this limit is the uncleared bush and trees. Between their houses you will perhaps see some plantain trees growing, and an occasional duck or
chicken or goat or dog straying about. Peter is
a little, short, gray-haired man, with a pleasant
face and a warm heart. He met me outside, and
led me into his cabin by the hand and sat me
down on a chair. Presently eight or ten women
came to the door to see 'Pauloo,' and said 'Bolo,'
and went away. He called in his little children,
nice little darkey fellows, clad in a string of beads
around the neck and two or three brass rings

around the ankles, that was all. The little fellows came between my knees, and leaned back on me very confidingly, which would not have been disagreeable if they had not just been rolling in the sand and ashes. Their mode of blessing any one is peculiar. If an old man in America wishes to show his kind feelings to a little boy, he puts his hands on his head and says, 'God bless you, my boy!' If an old African in like manner wishes to show his kind feelings towards any little fellow, he takes him by the shoulders and *spits* on the top of his head. This is with them expressive of all possible kindness.

"I visited the old king, Elepa, one day last week. He is an amiable old man, has four wives, and seems to live in peace. I found him attired in a white muslin sheet hanging loosely about him, and wrapped around his waist, extending down to his feet. He also wore a striped cotton cloth. When we went the old man was sitting outside the door of his bamboo reception house, but, without recognizing us when we approached him, he immediately arose and went in to the back part of the house and sat down. We followed him and sat down also near him. He then reached out his hands to shake hands with us, expecting us of course to get up and go to him. He then became very talkative and entertaining. His head wife was lying on a bamboo lounge beside him, asleep, so he waked her up, and seemed a little chagrined at her being asleep. She opened her eyes and talked to us, but did not get up. His legs were loaded with brass rings from the ankle almost to the knee.

"The king's house was only a single room, about twice as long as it was broad, with a floor of beaten clay, and open to the roof. The back wall was adorned with eight dusty pitchers, of two or three different shapes and colors, also two or three earthenware images, portable statues of Jack Spratt. There also he had a host of cheap woodcut pictures, great and small, but all highly colored, also looking-glasses, framed, and hung all around the walls. These, with a table, two or three chairs, and some bamboo benches or lounges, completed the furniture. About the centre was an upright post, which supports the ridge-pole of the roof. It also answered another purpose: to the bottom of it was attached a chain, which was to secure their prisoners of war and witches. The old king got his padlock and showed us how to secure them.

" *June* 8.—It has been some days since I had my pen in hand. My attack of fever returned again on the seventh day, and so I was laid aside. Part of the time I had a very hot fever, but for the greater part no especial sickness, only a feeling of intense weariness, and inability to do anything, with pains in back, limbs and head. The remedy is quinine, of which I have taken a great quantity. It seems strange that this land, which is as the garden of the earth for beauty and for its delightful climate, should have an atmosphere so full of deadly poison. In all my life I have never been in so delightful a climate, and the pleasantest season is just beginning to come. The air is always bracing; I have never yet felt it in the least oppressive. At night I find it very comfortable under a blanket. I do not think the sun is nearly so hot as at home, and we have double the quantity of cool, bracing air. Fruits we have in great plenty, many of which I have mentioned already.

"Everything moves along very pleasantly since Mr. Mackey's absence. Mrs. Mackey is a noble woman, very quiet, but keeps things moving like clock-work. Monday last was settlement day; we settle and square up with all employed once every four weeks. They are all greatly disposed to get their pay before they do the work, so that I have to hold some of them back a little.

"On Sabbath I went up and preached at Alongo. I did not have a very large congregation, nor do they ever turn out well unless you go round beforehand and tell them to come, and then very often they say 'Yes,' but have no intention of coming. After preaching at Alongo, I stopped on my way back at Nqume's town and preached there. Nqume is the head man—an old blind heathen. He said Mr. Clemens had been his friend. I told him I wanted him to be my friend also, and the old man held on to my hand with a long and warm grasp. I told him I wanted to preach for him, and soon all the people of the town that were about came together in his house—about twenty in all. They squatted down on stools and wherever they could find a seat, and then Uhamba (the young man who interpreted for me) and I sang a hymn. They were generally pretty quiet, while I preached of 'Christ coming into the world to save sinners.' Sometimes a woman, who did not know, perhaps, that she ought to keep quiet, would say something out loud; the rest would cry to her to 'hush,' and we would have silence immediately. The wife of Nqume, who is a nice woman, attentive and serious looking, said that once she tried to be a Christian, but not lately. I asked them all to come up to Alongo next Sabbath; they said they would, but I must come that way and let them know when it was Sabbath, which I willingly agreed to do. There are, I suppose, thirty or forty such little towns on the island, in most of which the missionaries have preached. Ah! if the Spirit would only come and open these dark minds and make the truth powerful, we should see displays of the glory of God that would make our hearts rejoice! Never can they be moved from this spiritual death until the Spirit of God shall do it in answer to fervent prayers here and at home.

"Yesterday was the day for giving out supplies to the mission, and you would scarcely suppose that our supplies here in Africa were the same as yours at home—flour, butter, rice, corn-starch, hams, kerosene oil, etc. Attending to this gives me quite a little bit of merchandising on Monday, and affords me exercise and diversion.

"I saw a beautiful flock of sheep at Alongo; Mr. Mackey has some here also, but you would scarcely take them for sheep in America. They are real sheep, however, except the wool, of which they have not a particle, but instead they have a beautiful, glossy coat of hair. Their skins look exactly like the skin of a young calf, and they are of every color—red, black and spotted. They would be a novelty in America.

"*Thursday*, June 16.—This evening I had promised Andiki, the native teacher who has charge of the school at Ugobi, to come up and preach there, so I mounted our pony at dusk and paced up along the beautiful white sandy beach about a mile and a half to the place. The ride was delightful, especially coming back, as it was a beautiful moonlight night, and the breeze was blowing fresh and balmy from the sea, and the tide was far out, which left a broad white beach. As I told you, there are no roads on the island except narrow footpaths, so that the only road is along the beach, and indeed there is no other needed, for all the little towns are built around the island near to the beach. As I got up before the time, I took a walk through one or two of the towns near by. The men and women were sitting about the doors of their cabins, and although I do not know that I had ever seen any of them before, almost all came to shake hands with me, saying 'Bolo, Pauloo.' As I had picked up a little of their language, I told them all to come to church, which they said they would do.

"At the usual hour Andiki rang his bell, and quite a little congregation gathered, forty or fifty in all; three of the women were professors of religion, and some others had been. They were very attentive while I preached. I preached to them about the *value* of their souls, and their *awful* state when lost, and tried to point out the way to save them. I expect to commence preaching next week around through their towns—it is not enough to preach only on the Sabbath. I pray that God may give me a terrible earnestness in my work here. I have been feeling, myself, most deeply, the truths that I preach to them about the *soul,* and I hope and pray that multitudes of them may be saved from a dreadful hell. It seems unaccountable to me, sometimes, that we can rest in peace for a moment, until we are sure that we and our friends have made sure work of our escape from the dreadful miseries of hell. Well assured am I, as that the sun shines, that all these terrible declarations in the Bible are true, and yet who would suspect, from the way in which we live, that we believed them? It is no easy matter to escape the flames. If our religion sits easy upon us, and our sins never trouble us, surely it is time to be alarmed."

In his journal of June 25 Mr. Paull writes:

"Press on to the kingdom—no looking back here—press right on, with courage firm and strong. Cut off the things that are behind; they are no longer ours; you have solemnly disowned them. Reach forth to the things that are before; they shall be your inheritance. You are a 'pilgrim and stranger.' Now, this land is not yours; you have no interest in it, nor in things about you; you are hurrying through, only tarrying for the night; to-morrow you journey on again. Be convinced of your 'pilgrim character,' let it sink into your heart, 'say it' in all your life; for they that say such things declare plainly that they *seek* a country—that they are pressing on hard after it, careless of all that is behind, 'unmindful of the country whence they came out.'

"There can be no such thing as *earnest* pressing on to the kingdom while our eyes are turned backward; they must be thoroughly and eagerly fixed on the kingdom to which we move. Lot's wife was fleeing to the mountains, while her eyes and her heart were yearning for Sodom; this was no escaping from destruction, this was 'staying in Sodom;' and she perished by the way. As the plough moves, our hands must be upon it, and our eyes and our thoughts must go with it; if not, then we are not fit for the work, and our life is a lie. 'No man, having put his hand to the plough and looking back, is fit for the kingdom of God.' O Saviour! how shall we ever reach thy kingdom, unless thou wilt knit our souls to thine, unless thou wilt lift up our *whole beings,* and centre them *intensely* upon thyself?"

Here we see the workings of Mr. Paull's inner life, how ardently he desired entire consecration to Christ and his service. No wonder that one whose heart burned with such longings for complete consecration to his work should be willing to encounter perils by sea and by land to repeat the story of the cross to the perishing in Africa.

Under the same date he writes to his sister:

"About a week since we despatched our mails, and already I have begun to write again for the next. This is to save me the perplexity of crowding all my letter-writing together at the last. And then, too, every day as it glides along may have some little incidents which, if not gathered up as they pass, will be pressed aside by others and forgotten. But you will not look for much variety now, as, instead of being tossed on the tide, I am becoming settled in life, and my duties and diversions are gradually falling into their daily regular round. Almost the only changes, too, one feels called on to note in so small and unimportant a world as ours is here, are his own ever-varying moods within, or the success or failure of his plans with reference to others without. These, while they are always fraught with absorbing interest to himself, are generally of but little importance to others. But I will always write, taking it for granted that what I write will be at least of some interest at home. I begin to see now how it is that, of all things for a man, solitude is sometimes the best. When he is cut off from the world without, he begins to explore more diligently and to become better acquainted with the world within. He begins to find that there is a vast unknown there, filled with mysteries of which he had never dreamed. If a man is driven to look much within, he will see strange sights and hear strange sounds, and shrink away from beholding many a gloomy, fearful picture. His life, too, may become a strange mixture of gloom and gladness, and continual interchanging of sunlight and shadow. But all this would be to any man a rich and royal blessing, a princely gift at the hands of God, tending to make one wiser and purer and truer. Natures such as ours can never be cleansed

9

from their dross without passing through some sort of fire.

"*June* 28.—One part of a day since I last wrote I spent pleasantly reading, etc., down in a little rocky cave by the sea amid the incessant roar of the waves and dashing of the spray. I love to sit there in my leisure hours and read and think while all is so secluded and quiet—no noise save the thunder of the surf as it breaks on the shore. Occasionally I lift up my eyes in this quiet nook (it faces the sun), and look away to the westward, trying to arrange in my mind a picture of things as they may be at home.

"Most of my days, however, I spend in my bamboo house, studying, reading, writing, etc., or, when not doing that, attending to the business of the mission, which occasionally takes several hours of the day. This morning, for instance, I spent sending off a big boat to Iloby—an island near where some traders have their factories—loaded with twenty-five pine chests, which the boys working in the shops had made. These chests we exchange with the traders for supplies, and they sell them to the natives.

"One day last week I got on the pony (Charley), and taking Uhamba, went away four or five miles off on the other side of the island, to visit some towns that belong to my charge at Alongo. I was at five or six towns, and preached at one and invited all of the people to come to church, which they said they would do. But, unfortunately, they think it but little harm to tell a lie, and so, when Sabbath came, they had forgotten their promise. I do not think they can be reached without going to their towns and preaching to them there, and I intend to do this, though I believe it has not been customary. The people were all glad to see me, and the women clattered away with their tongues, each seeming to try who could speak the loudest. Many said, 'He is like Mr. Clemens;' and then their usual message was that they wanted me to be good to them. At one of the towns about a dozen of the men and women followed me down to the beach, and told Uhamba that they wanted me to let them see Charley run; so I gave him a little gallop, and they stood and watched, as much pleased as children with Charley's nimbleness.

"This was a very pleasant day's ride to me, both on account of seeing the people and some parts of the island that I had not seen before. Quite a number of pretty little squirrels crossed my path, something like our ground-squirrels, but a little larger;

also some beautiful birds of a deep rich blue color, and one African dove which was beautiful in shape and size and gentleness of appearance, like our own, but of a darker color on the back, with the under part of its neck and breast white. About most of the towns I see a little flock of goats and of hairy, spotted sheep. The children know Charley all over the island, and often the first noise that I would hear on coming near a town would be from some of the children that had caught a glimpse of him, with their noisy greeting, 'Oh, Charley! Oh, Charley !'

"I had my sermon already prepared for preaching at Alongo on the next day (this was Saturday); but as I rode along, that text, 'God so loved the world that he gave his only begotten Son,' etc., came into my mind so fully, and with such comfort to myself, that I determined to take it, and prepared a sermon and came home and preached it the next day. Uhamba, who is a member of the church, interprets for me when I preach. My other interpreter is a suspended church member, and has been guilty of several grievous sins; so that I do not think it is right, either for his sake or the gospel's, to allow him to meddle with so sacred a business. He says, however, that he is praying and wishes to repent and return to his profession. I hope he is sincere.

"Uhamba is a very decent fellow, and wears a clean shirt and a pair of pants, which is full dress; but when he came on Sabbath morning to go with me, I noticed that he had on a filthy shirt that he had worked in a week, perhaps, and a dirty piece of gingham wrapped about him, reaching from his waist to his feet. I thought it very strange, but found that a friend of his had died the night before, and that this is the African badge of mourning—to go as *dirty* as you possibly can.

"I had a good congregation at Alongo, though not the tenth of those that promised to come. I had a great deal of freedom in preaching. On my way back I preached at Iduma's town. He is one of the rich men on the island, and has about twenty wives. I preached to him and most of his wives with all the earnestness and solemnity that I had, and I trust they felt some of the truths that were spoken. They seemed very solemn and attentive. I have a confident expectation of seeing many of these dark children of sin yet coming to Christ, and the thought greatly encourages me, for it is God's work and his arm is not shortened, and he has bidden us

pray and wait and expect a blessing; and if we
do these things, why should we not expect it, not
timidly, but *firmly?*"

Here is a letter of Mr. Paull's to his younger
brother which will give some idea of Africa and
of heathen life:

"Corisco, June 30, 1864.

"I have been looking for a letter from you telling me that you have been studying hard all winter and were anxious to be at it again, and that
you were determined to be a fine scholar and a
noble and good man. I know that you do study
well and faithfully, and it has made me proud of
you and given me high hopes that I shall one day
be prouder yet of what you will be and do. You
will not let me be disappointed. You must settle
it first of all in your mind, if you wish to become
a true and noble man, that you will not be ashamed
to be *good,* even if every one around you laughs
and sneers. You are not to care for what any one
says, if you know that you are doing right, any
more than you care for the bark of a dog. Deter-
mine, then, in your own mind, *now,* that you will
be kind to everybody, and that you will try to love
everybody and do everybody some good, even if
it puts you to inconvenience; that you will neither

do nor think anything under any consideration that you know to be wrong; that nobody shall make you ashamed to read the Bible often, and to pray often, and to think often about God. If you do these things, you will become a true and a noble man, and I do sincerely pray that you may never be anything else; and so you must begin *now.* Go every day to some quiet place, and there kneel down and solemnly give your heart to God and ask him to come and make it his home. You and Jim are daily in my thoughts and also in my prayers, and I hope that you do not forget to pray for me also.

"Yesterday I had a little trip that I suppose would have interested and delighted you, if you had been here. In the morning Dr. Nassau came to my study and said that he and Mrs. M'Queen and the schoolgirls (for it was vacation) were going round to the other side of the island in the afternoon to gather shells, and asked me to go along. So we started about 1 o'clock, the doctor on foot, for he prefers walking, Mrs. M'Queen in a hammock slung by a pole lying across two men's shoulders: this is a very common way of traveling in Africa; I went on Charley. He and I have become quite close friends, and we generally go together.   He is an affectionate little fellow, but sometimes I have to box his ears for biting me, as he loves to *nip* everybody that comes in his way, and scarcely one of the natives will go within a rod of him.   We went along the beach until we came to Ugobi, and then we took one of the native footpaths that run through the bush across the island.   After winding along the path for a while and crossing a marshy creek or two, suddenly we came on to the most refreshing spot I have seen in Africa.   It was a long, narrow meadow, level as a floor and covered with green grass.   It was about a mile long and from about one hundred to three hundred yards wide.   Beautiful palms and other trees lined it all along on either side.   As we rode through it I almost fancied that the next turn would bring us to some beautiful dwelling with all the accompaniments of civilized life, for this little meadow has such a thoroughly civilized appearance in comparison with the wild bush that is around us everywhere else.   When we got to the end of the meadow, we came again upon the seashore, at the spot to which we were going, and a beautiful, broad, white sandy beach it was.   From it we could see the mainland and Iloby and another little island.   While we gathered sea-shells, which lay

thick along the shore, scores of parrots flew scream-
ing over our heads, and occasionally a large eagle
would swoop down and sail just a little bit over
our heads, while cranes and gulls and other sea-
birds waded about in the edge of the water or
sailed around in the air above us.   After spending
an hour or two and gathering a good many shells,
we came back a good deal wearied.   The shells
that the girls gathered Mrs. M'Queen gave me to
increase my stock, and you may perhaps see some
of them one day.

"We have a few white men come to see us occasionally, and they all like to come here, for there
is scarcely any place along the coast that looks so
homelike and comfortable, and when there are
any sick men at Iloby or on any vessels that come
about here, they are generally sent to Corisco for
Mr. Mackey and Dr. Nassau to cure up.   We had
three or four visitors from Iloby the other day:
they took dinner and went away again.   One was
young Watson, who came out with me in the Elgiva; another was a Dutch captain by the name of
Henert — quite a pleasant fellow.   He told an
anecdote of one of our Corisco black men that he
had seen somewhere to show how they make mis-
takes sometimes.   Peter (the black man) is an old

man, and has a son called Bobe. Bobe had been away somewhere; and supposing Captain Henert might have seen him or known something about him, the old man said, 'Did you see my father, Bobe?' 'Why,' said Captain Henert, 'you are an old man and Bobe is a young man; Bobe cannot be your *father:* he must be your *son.*' 'Oh yes,' said the old man; 'well, now I think that is it—yes, he my son Bobe.' This, however, is only a mistake of the poor old heathen: there is no harm in that; and perhaps there is nothing wrong in being amused at it. But there are some things said and done by the heathen that bring no pleasant feelings—drive away everything, indeed, but grief and sorrow.

"I told you some time ago of two or three persons on the island who had been killed under suspicion of having bewitched some man that had died. Now there is another old man about to die who has asked the people, in case he dies, to kill some one on suspicion of having bewitched him. This is the father of Andiki, one of the native preachers. And yesterday, too, although it is almost too revolting to speak of, a man that lives right by here came to the house and asked Mrs. Mackey for some poison to give to his mother.

He said she had been sick a long time and would not get well, and that he had to stay at home and take care of her, and he did not want to be so closely confined, but wanted to get away. Dr. Nassau saw him afterward and talked to him, but he said that he did not know that that was anything the white man thought wrong. So you see how pitiable a thing it is to be a heathen. They have no government here, no laws, no courts to try and sentence criminals, no officers to punish them. Every man does as he pleases, and they indulge in almost every sin and commit almost every crime. Do you think you could spend your life in any more useful way than by coming out here, after a while, to teach these poor people how to live and how to die? Keep this object before you while you study, and ask God to make you fit to tell these people, who are so miserable, how they may be happy. This would be far better and make you far happier than living a life of sin, or a life of pleasure, or spending your life in making money. I want you and Jim both to be missionaries. Think of it often, and settle it in your minds that, if God will send you, you will go. I know of no way in which you could do more good."

Mr. Paull's next letter was to his father, and, written on the anniversary of our national independence, it contains a few thoughts in reference to that memorable event.

"Corisco, July 4, 1864.

"I do not remember certainly that I have written to you individually since I left Scotland. My letters heretofore have been in journal form, and rather intended for all than for any one in particular, and even yet I think I will jot down things usually in the same way, just as they happen, or as thoughts occur to me; but this time I have departed from my ordinary plan.

"The 4th of July calls up many recollections that are pleasant and many faces that are familiar, and my fancy carries me to where I seem to see you all honoring the day, perhaps by some social reunion, it may be a family 'pic-nic,' or joining in some more public celebration. Here it passes away as other days, save that we each one remember it, and take pride in it as a day of gladness at home, but otherwise there is nothing outward to mark it. I have spent most of the day in attending to the business of the station, settling up with the men employed, which is done monthly, giving out supplies from the storehouse, having our boats painted, etc. I usually give Mondays to the business of the station, and an hour on other days, when it is necessary. Dr. Nassau has even considerably more business than I have of this kind. We were also at the funeral of an *old headman* to-day who was buried in our graveyard because of his son's having been connected with the mission; he was still a heathen, however. We did not allow any of the heathen ceremonies at the grave, but Dr. Nassau prayed and made a short address.

"We have been on the anxious lookout all day for the mail, as this was the day on which we certainly expected it, but there is no sign of it yet, and we begin to give up all hope until to-morrow or next day. This is one of our greatest disappointments here, when the mail fails us at the time when we expect it.

"Yesterday I sat down for the first time with the native Christians here as they gathered around the table of the Lord. There were not very many of them, perhaps twenty in all, and three of them were coming for the first time; once there were many more, but, alas! one and another has turned away into sin; and this is the saddest part of all the missionary work, to see the devil lead captive and triumph over those who once seemed to be free from his fetters. At the communion seasons, which occur every three months, all of the members, both on the island and at the stations on the mainland, are expected to be present, and the whole number, I think, is near seventy. But many of them for various reasons were kept away this time. Dr. Nassau conducted the services; I preached the preparatory sermon on the day before. I do not see any special features of encouragement in the work here now—indeed, several things almost make it have a gloomy aspect, especially the fewness of our numbers in the mission, the falling away of some of the native members and a general coldness and indifference on the part of most, though I have sometimes, when hope was buoyant, been tempted to look on these things as almost encouraging, for God generally chooses a time to work when the glory will be manifestly all due to himself. It seems to be such a time now, for if light and life and strength spring up out of this darkness and death and weakness, all must surely fill their mouths with songs of praise and say, 'It is of the Lord; to him alone be all the glory for ever. Amen.'

"*Tuesday*, 5th.—This afternoon I spent very

pleasantly among my Alongo people. After riding about three and a half miles I stopped at one of the little towns and talked with the people, telling them that I would preach for them if they would call in some more people from one or two towns near by, which they did, and I had a very nice little congregation. They were very attentive to all I said to them of 'God's love in sending his Son to die for sinners lost and wretched.' Some of them listened with most fixed attention. I noticed a great talking among them after preaching, and Uhamba told me they were saying, 'That was a true word that was told them.' This evening the mail came that we had been so anxiously looking for, and we opened it with eager hands to get at the precious contents of news from home and friends, for so far as earthly pleasures are concerned here, our letters from home are the greatest.

"I begin to feel entirely at home in Africa now, and am altogether contented and happy in the work. My health is very good, and, so far as we can judge, my constitution promises to be of the kind that may bear the climate well. I shall heartily rejoice if this be so. I believe that God has sent me here, and I hope for good. If he is my guide, I shall be safe; and I desire to be done for ever with attempting to direct my own steps, as I fear I have sometimes done in the time that is past.

"I am collecting some little African curiosities, which I will send home, as they will be of some interest to you all. Among other things I have some brass and copper ankle-rings and some beads which I bought from an African princess. Mrs. M'Queen was down at Mrs. Mackey's to sit a while this evening, and says she has discovered that I have a namesake on the island. Some heathen mother that I have never seen has called her baby after me; 'Pauloo' is its name—that is, its English name. Its native name is *Ubengi*, after the interpreter; he, I believe, is its uncle. Mrs. M'Queen has been down pretty often to give Mrs. Mackey a word of cheer in her loneliness, and it is well. I have a great respect for Mrs. Mackey. She is calm and even-tempered. Grace in her seems to shine out clearly as it is gradually ripening her for glory. Her lamp, I think, is always trimmed and burning. There is nothing on earth so beautiful as a character mellowed by grace until it seems almost divine.

"*July* 15.—We have had a young Scotch trader

here from Iloby for several days. He came over sick, but has gone away to-day quite well again. This is a hospital for all the sick sailors and traders in the neighborhood; they come here to be cured up. I was around to-day on another missionary tour beyond Alongo. I only had time to preach in one town; started after dinner, and reached home again about six o'clock. It was a long walk for *Uhamba*—seven or eight miles—but he seemed just as fresh when we came back as when we started.

"The church at home is growing fast, I hope, under Mr. Fife's care. I trust he may be blessed greatly, and I see not why *there* as well as elsewhere (for I see notices of many revivals) Zion may not be built in these troublous times. There are very many in the congregation who have grown up under the holy influence of a family altar, and they ought to come out and declare themselves on the side of Christ. To resist the constant, gentle wooing influences of the Spirit as they are shed abroad daily in every pious, prayerful home seems a dark and reckless sin—a sin that I do not think will be lightly judged in the latter day, for God is very jealous of the treatment that his Holy Spirit shall receive; and to have him mocked and set at naught is to treat the Spirit of God as the Jews did his Son.　It is worth more than a birthright to a throne to have been brought up in a pious home.　I shall never cease to be grateful for all the holy and restraining influences that were thrown around me.　They follow one every day that he lives, and they never cease to do their part in shaping the life and in forming it for God.　It is not in vain to sow the seed and to water it with much prayer; surely the harvest will come at last.

"I saw some parties settling a dispute the other day in a way which was rather novel.　As they have no courts, no regular laws, no officers of justice, usually might is right.　But sometimes friends from both parties meet and settle the matter pretty satisfactorily.　Generally, however, when a man thinks he is wronged by another, he sends an ambassador to say that he must have so much pay or he will come with his friends and fight.　If the person to whom this message is sent happens to be a weaker person in point of friends, he has no resort but to pay the demand.　Ibape, one of our workmen, came to me the other day greatly distressed and said that a man had a '*palaver*' with him, and was going to come and fight him if he did not pay the demand. He was obliged to pay (I believe it was just enough in this case), and came to me to get help. A very usual demand is the price of a slave, which is a set value, and consists of just so many things of different kinds, and must be neither more nor less (they amount in all to about thirty dollars), and these things constitute currency. The price of a slave is twelve romals (cloth), one gun, one keg of powder, one iron pot, two iron bars, two brass rods, two heads of tobacco, one shirt, one red cap, two gun-flints, one fire-steel, one cutlass, one small bell, one pine chest, one stone jar, two tobacco pipes. All of these articles must be included, and must be neither more nor less; nor must anything else, even though it be of equal or greater value, be substituted in the place of any of the articles in the list.

"*July* 19.—We have heard nothing lately about the plans of the Spanish, and so do not know whether they intend to let us stay here or not; perhaps they will—at least until they get thoroughly under way.

"I found my little congregation at Alongo considerably enlarged on Sunday. I think going about among their towns has had a good effect on them. I hope they may come on until there will

not be room enough to hold them. I preached on
my way back at one of the native towns, and had
a good little congregation. I have had a strong,
unwavering confidence in God that he will yet ere
long work wonders among the people here. Pray
much for me and for the success of the gospel
among the people. I often feel most grateful to
God that he has yet spared you that I may have
the benefit of your prayers: surely I need them.
It was just one year yesterday since I preached my
farewell sermon at Morrison (Illinois). It has
soon passed away; another and another will go as
quickly. I often look back with great pleasure to
my stay at Morrison. It was the most anxious six
months I ever spent, and yet in many respects the
most happy, and, I believe, decidedly the most useful. God most surely designed that I should come
here. I look back and see the path most strangely
marked out. From the time I thought of the mission work one difficulty and another was gradually
taken out of the way, and then by some most
marked providences it was kept from being
blocked up again.

"I feel that this is my proper sphere, and I
hope to be blessed in the work. My health is
good—perhaps has never been better. I feel as yet

no lassitude, as I thought I should; sometimes I feel a little depression of spirits, which I had been free from for the last four or five years, but perhaps when I get at the work thoroughly this may pass away. I am glad that I have the opportunity of preaching some as I study the language. I feel that I am at my proper work only when I am preaching. I expect to keep up the habit of preaching in the towns at least one day in the week besides the Sabbath. If I did not do this, I should feel depressed with the thought that I was doing nothing, and I seem to be doing almost nothing as it is.

"I think I see uncle, doctor and the boys busy at the hay, as this is harvest-time at home. I wish you could have as cool and pleasant weather for harvesting as we have here. This is the African winter, and the natives go about shivering; so do the white people that have been here any length of time. Good-bye for another month, and may our God bless and keep us all!"

"*July* 27. (*Journal.*)—There are seasons in the lives of some Christians—and they seem to be periodical—when 'the enemy comes in like a flood' (expressive figure!), the flood gates are up and the rushing tide of corruption sweeps everything before it.

Of what avail is a helpless sinner's strength in such a time as this? All good resolutions bend like rushes, and the flood-tide sweeps over them. A Saviour's free and boundless grace for the chief of sinners is the only hiding-place."

To his mother:

"Corisco, July 27, 1864.

"I scarcely had intended to commence writing letters until after our mail came, but as I sat down by my table this evening with my lighted candle before me, my books about me and feeling quite comfortable in my solitude, it came into my mind that I might spend a few minutes very pleasantly in writing to you.

"I have been busy for the last two days, and expect to be for another, putting a roof on the church. I can hardly say that *I* have been very busy, however, as my work was not very difficult. I have had eight or nine *barefooted* and *barelegged*, and some of them *bareheaded*, men to look after as they sat along in a row on the top of the church smoking a short pipe or two, out of which each took a whiff in turn. They chatter away as fast as they can, and work pretty well while you stand before them and look on, but almost the moment one turns his back the work stops, and very likely the whole row, or at least a part, turns over on its back to rest. They work for about sixteen cents a day, and really do as well as could be expected of them when one thinks of their irregular and indolent life. The roofing material is of palm leaves pinned together with little sticks into mats about five or six feet long by two wide. These mats, overlapping each other, are tied on to the bamboo rafters with long limber splits, something like those used to hang bacon. These mats make a pretty complete roof, which turns the rain very well for two or three years. I have one or two other jobs of roofing to do yet—the boat-house and part of the dwelling-house—and some fences to make before the rainy season commences; this will finish the out-door work.

"The comparison of the righteous to the palm tree in the Psalms seems more beautiful and forcible since I came here than ever before. Both for beauty and for use it seems to surpass almost all other trees. The natives build their houses almost from top to bottom with it. They make twine for their nets from its fibre. They get their wine from it by tapping the tree. They lie under its shade and drink the delicious cocoanut milk (I speak of two varieties of the palm which we have here, the cocoanut and the oil palm), and they use the oil of the nut for food and for light. The heart of the tree also makes most delicious cabbage. We, too, know the value of the palm for food. Yesterday, for instance, we made our dinners on palm butter and palm cabbage, and bread fruit, plantains, rice and sweet potatoes, etc. The palm butter is a choice dish made of palm nuts and chicken boiled together. The palm cabbage (so called from its resemblance to cabbage) is the heart of the palm tree taken out near the bottom; it is very good, but it kills the tree to get it. This that we had yesterday was the first that I have ever seen. It was sent to Mrs. Mackey by Mrs. M'Queen. Mrs. M'Queen had received a quantity of it as a present from the Spanish priest, who is a gentlemanly young fellow and disposed to be polite.

"*August* 8.—For more than a week we have been turning our eyes seaward in hopes of catching a glimpse of our coming mail, but now we have almost given up the expectation for this month, as we think it would have been here before this if there had been an opportunity to send it down from Fernando Po. Two of the graces that one needs, especially in Africa, are patience and quiet submission. If these are strong, they will make many a rough place smooth.

"As this is Monday, it has been my day for giving out supplies, but the labor was very light. I opened a barrel of butter, and I have not been more surprised at anything than that we should have such excellent butter every day away out here. It is sent out to us packed in small kegs, six of which are put in each barrel. I think nothing else is done to preserve it, except filling the barrel with strong brine.

"*August* 9.—To-day I have been busy with six men making fence around the garden. It is not a very difficult process, but a little tedious. Long sticks are first sharpened and put into the ground one foot apart. These are the posts, and the rails are bamboo poles which are tied to the posts with long timber splits. We make the fence about six feet high, and it answers every purpose while it lasts, but the hot suns and drenching rains rot it away in one year. There is scarcely any wood on the island fit for fencing; it is all soft and easily rots. The pickets for the fence which runs all around the mission grounds were brought from the mainland, as is also the wood which Mrs. Mackey burns. The large timber on Corisco is not very abundant, although there are some immense trees which I think would measure thirty or forty feet in circumference. The women cut away most of the trees, or the tops of them, when they make their *farms*, which are only about half-acre gardens. When they choose a place for a *farm*, they take away the underbrush and only cut the limbs off the trees, so that the tree may not die; and after they have used the ground for a year or two the soil is exhausted, and they leave it to grow up again with bushes and trees, so that it may recover its strength.

"At this season of the year (the dry season) the women spend most of their time making farms and planting cassada and plantains: on these they chiefly live. They do nearly all their work with a simple iron cutlass, which is something like a corn-cutter, or rather like a sabre. Their farms are often a long way off from their houses, and they pack their produce home in baskets, which rest on the small of the back and are supported by a band reaching up to the front part of the head. They carry immense loads in this way, the weight of which rests mainly on the head, and it is bent forward as they walk. They carry their wood in this way, tied in large bundles and stuck endwise into the basket, also their water, which is first put into large four or five-gallon jugs and the jug is put into the basket. This dry season is their time for working, and I suppose they lounge in their huts when the rains come. Now they have it perfectly dry, scarcely a drop of rain in the whole four months that the season lasts.

"As I walk about the beach I see them improving the dry season to boil their salt. They put up a little shed and cover it with palm leaf mats, and under this they lounge many a day boiling salt and roasting palm nuts and plantains and fish. Their kettles seem to be large pieces of copper beaten into some kind of shape for holding water. They never look happier than when they are lying round the fire roasting plantains and boiling salt. The women, I suppose, are the better portion of the people; and yet I do not know, either, for they have so little in their characters that is *womanly* that you scarcely can persuade yourself to give them the place that otherwise would be their due.

"*August* 10.—Part of my men went away this morning—one went a fishing and another somewhere else. Scarcely any of them have patience to work three or four days at the same thing. But if one goes, half a dozen are ready in a minute to take his place. They are all anxious to work for a day or so, to get some fish-hooks or cloth or something else. This season of the year is a fine time with them for fishing. They go out in their boats to sea, a distance of two or three miles, and spend the day catching what they call bianga (a fish about as large as a mackerel) with hook and line. Each man will catch perhaps twenty. They cannot preserve them long except by salting them heavily and then smoking them, which they do by simply hanging them up in their houses, for they have no chimneys. They build the fire in the middle of the house and let it blaze and smoke away; the smoke and soot do not disturb them in the least. In anything connected with boating or fishing I believe they are tolerably expert. Their boats are made out of immense trees, and are hewn out into excellent shape, very much like a skiff. They use sails on them, sometimes one, sometimes two. Even the little boys are passionately fond of boats and the water. They make very handsome little boats, rigged with sails, and then their chief amusement is in wading along the beach and dragging them in the water.

"If nothing providential hinders I expect to

start on Tuesday to visit the stations on the mainland and preach to the people there. The out-
stations are occupied by *Scripture readers,* who hold
prayer-meetings and make exhortations. It was
the intention of the mission for some one of the
missionaries to visit these stations once a month,
but this has not been done of late because of the
smallness of our force. Dr. Nassau is so much
troubled with sea-sickness when he sails that it is
almost impossible for him to leave the island; besides, his other duties—of school, etc.—make his
hands full. So I have offered to take the work at
the out-stations until more help comes. Dr. Nassau is a fine singer and very fond of music. He
teaches all the children under his care to sing.
Many of the natives who have been about the mission sing very well, and even start quite a number
of tunes. When I preach, I generally depend on
my interpreter to raise the tunes.

"Dr. Nassau is expecting his wife out again before long. She seems to be very active and ener-
getic, and has a share in doing everything that is
to be done. She is fond of gardening, and has in-
stilled quite a love for the art into the doctor. He
has a fine large garden of sweet potatoes, which are
easily cultivated. The whole process consists in

throwing up some ridges of earth and breaking off some pieces of green potato vine and sticking them in, and in a few weeks you have a flourishing crop. Indeed, they grow all around wherever a piece of vine is thrown down.

"Our farm here is not large, perhaps three acres in all, but with the amount of stock on it—viz., a horse, two cattle, twenty goats and half a dozen sheep—we have a good deal of trouble as well as on larger farms, but not in *providing food*. All that is necessary is simply to let them run and feed on the grass all the year round. It grows very rank, and a little piece of ground will produce a great deal. It is never safe to let a sheep or a goat outside the enclosure, as it is almost sure to be stolen. Even the cattle of the missionaries at Gaboon are pretty sure to be speared by the natives when they wander away from the mission grounds.

"*August* 13.—My last letter from home was dated 29th of March, wellnigh five months ago, and we are still in ignorance of home affairs. For lack of anything later, and for sake of bringing up *home pictures* more vividly, last night I took out the letters that I have received from home since I left and re-read them. This was at least some satisfaction. Five have reached me in all. One of the continual temptations here is to have one's thoughts running backward to home and friends perhaps more than is right. The reasons are, first, that one has no social enjoyments here, and it is hard to root out the natural craving after friends and friendly intercourse; and since the craving cannot be satisfied with the reality, one is constantly tempted to be reaching backward after the shadow or the remembrance of what was. Then, also, the utter absence of outward business and stir and excitement to draw off the attention has the effect of turning one's thoughts altogether inward, there to be occupied in studying one's thoughts and feelings and experiences, or else in running back over the memories of the past, gathering out the bright spots for good cheer, and ruminating over the darker ones to learn some lesson for the future. I try, however, to bring my dreaming within certain bounds, and do but little of it at other times, unless occasionally when the tide breaks over all bounds and takes its course.

"But aside from all this, I am perfectly content in my African home, and would not give up my field of labor here for any that I have had, or might hope to have, in my own land. I say this from the feeling that it is my proper place, and that God has sent me here in answer to prayer and a sincere desire that I might be placed just where my life might tell most truly for good and for God's glory. Certainly, in the economy of God, there is a place for every child of his, to which he is in every way better adapted than to any other, and in which he will accomplish more than in any other. He made none of us without some design. He had some end to accomplish in the creation of each one of us; and if we seek earnestly and submissively and prayerfully to have him fulfill his whole will in us, we shall never be disappointed, and in the end God shall surely be glorified.

"One of the most important effects on myself that I look for here, and sincerely desire, is that my worldliness may be in some measure subdued—I mean my fondness for society and pleasure of a social kind. It seems in all my past life to have had possession of me like a demon, almost, and to have hurried me along under its mad sway. And yet so weak am I that if subjected to the same temptations, unless kept by the mighty power of God, I should be hurried away as madly again. Every man in his best unaided strength is like a reed before the blast; he bends and shakes until the storm is past, and when the next wind blows he bends and shakes again. They are blessed above all others who mind religion in the earliest dawn of life; they are saved from many a snare and from many a sorrow for time spent in folly.

"Since coming to Corisco I have seen but little that is rare of the animal or reptile kind. There is not much variety in that way on Corisco. Lizards, it is true, run about on all sides and under your feet, and birds in great variety—and some of them, too, very beautiful—fly all around, and little squirrels jump about within a few yards of you. There are also some snakes, but I have seen only a few. To-day, as the spring is about failing (they always do here in the dry season), I opened the large cistern, so that we could use the water in it. Two snakes had found their way into it before us; one was dead and putrid, the other alive and sprightly. They were five or six feet long, and seemed to be a variety of the cobra di capello, and are very poisonous. The living one I soon put an end to with the cutlass. These are, I think, the only snakes that I have seen on the island.

"*Monday,* August 14.—Yesterday I preached as usual at Alongo and in one of the towns near by. My congregations have been steadily increasing, and give me great encouragement both by their quietness and attention and by the numbers that come. This makes me hopeful that by preaching to them patiently, earnestly and prayerfully their hearts may yet be reached. I spend one day in every week going around among their towns to preach and invite them to church. There is no desire among them to hear the gospel, as is often supposed in America. They are too deeply buried in darkness and in sin to know or feel their need of it. But this, instead of being a reason for withholding the gospel, is only the stronger argument for pressing and urging it upon them, 'compelling them to come in.' Most of them, when urged to come, make the promise to come simply to get rid of you, or else they allow some trifling excuse to keep them away. The older ones, who are attached to their customs and heathenish practices, say that it is better to stay away and to keep their wives away, for they do not want to become Christians, and that if they go to church they would be very apt to do so. But I am persuaded that, stubborn as the natural heart is, multitudes will yet bend their necks to the sway of Him whose yoke is easy and whose burden is light.

"We had a short visit to-day from three or four traders on Iloby. Some of them are very nice, gentlemanly young Scotchmen, who have come out to this coast for sake of the higher salaries given by their employers in Scotland. One was a handsome young fellow with a fine noble face, but very pale. His name, Maclachlan. He came to consult the doctor about his health, and had fears of consumption, but the doctor relieved his fears and told him there was no particular danger. He put three dollars into my hand as he went away for the benefit of the mission. It makes me sorry to see a fine young fellow come out here as a trader, because almost certain ruin is the result. There are no restraints of society, no wholesome influence of any kind, while on the other hand they have every opportunity to run into all possible excess and to indulge every appetite and passion. Many a noble young Scotchman along this coast has fallen a shattered wreck before he reached mature manhood, and his bones lie mouldering under the sands.

"I have promised to spend next Sabbath at Iloby and preach there on my way back from the mainland. I would that I could be instrumental in doing them some good! There are five or six of them there now, and one of them was anxious to have me come and preach to them, as he said they had no Sabbath at all there now, but that Sabbath was their greatest trade-day. The factories of the traders of which you read in Du Chaillu are simply stores in which they keep goods—viz., clothes, beads, rum, tobacco, etc.—to trade to the natives for dyewoods, India rubber, ivory, palm oil, etc., which they send back to England and Scotland. There is indeed quite an extensive trade all along this coast. Ships pass within sight of us almost every week, and sometimes several in a week.

"I have never mentioned in any of my letters, I think, the use I made of Mrs. M'Dowell's contribution. Let her know that it was invested in Bibles, which were presented to four little boys in Alongo school. They are learning to read them, and I hope she will add her fervent prayers that they may also learn to obey them; and doubtless the day will come that they will rise up and call her blessed. I wish that many more would follow her example. Many a dollar might be given that would never be missed by the giver, and yet if prayer, earnest and believing prayer, went with it, it would kindle a light in some soul which would at last blend its rays with the light that is uncreated. A soul plucked from this darkness and planted in the light, there to shine for ever calm and beautiful as a star—that would be a rare reward for a little self-denial. I have thought much of late that I could ask no higher gift of God for me than that I might be so wrapped up in a desire for his glory and for the good of this people as that I should bend every thought and every energy, while I live, to this end. But, alas! it is with me as I suppose it is with many others: I have exalted conceptions of what I would like to do and like to be, but my progress toward the mark is slow. I only seem to sit and resolve, and then let the matter end, though I hope it is not altogether so.

"For the last two or three weeks my progress in the study of the Benga has been slow. Building fence and roofing the church were interruptions, but it was necessary that these should be done while the dry season lasted, and my interpreter for the last week has not come. His brother, the headman of the town, has lately died, and his excuse is that since then much business falls on him. It is possible that we may have to dissolve partnership. I had hoped that our letters would get here before I left for the mainland, but there is no sign of their reaching us."

To his mother and sister :

"CORISCO, August 23, 1864.

" I am safely back again from my journey to the mainland. It was very pleasant, and the wearisomeness seemed as nothing because of the delightfulness of the work. On Tuesday, 16th, after due preparation for a week's boating, I got off on my first preaching tour to the mainland. The preparation kept me busy all the morning—that is, getting the men (six in number) ready, getting the boat launched, the mast up and the sails ready, etc., and then, too, getting some shawls for sleeping on and under (for there are no beds on the mainland), and overcoats, and extra clothing for emergencies, and a stock of medicines also in case of sickness. Then also some cloth and knives, etc., must be taken along to buy food for the men ; also some supplies for the Scripture readers whom I went to visit. Besides these, my own larder had to be stocked ; for there is no white man's food there, unless it be an occasional chicken. Mrs. Mackey presided over this part, and stocked a small box for me with roast beef, and chicken, and crackers, and cakes, and bread, with the necessary helps in eating, viz., knife and fork, plate, towels, etc., also a candle or two and some matches. Thus comfortably equipped, I started off near noon with my crew of six and two or three passengers.

"Our boat skimmed along the water before a good breeze beautifully as a bird. It is only an open boat, very much like a large skiff, perhaps thirty feet or more long; very strong it is, and will carry a heavy load. We had not traveled very far until I felt my old squeamishness returning, and as the best preventive I laid down on my back and shut my eyes. This plan would have succeeded, I think, but presently some of the men called out that they had brought nothing to bail out water with; and as the water was coming in, I was obliged to get up and search my box for something that would answer, and fortunately found a small tin bucket filled with cakes which could easily be emptied. But the getting up unsettled my stomach, and I was seasick—sick enough indeed. But it was soon over, at least the worst of it, and an hour or two more of sailing brought us to Big Eloby, our first stopping-place.

"Big Eloby and Little Eloby are small islands directly east of Corisco, twelve miles from it and within four miles of the mainland. Little Eloby is perhaps one and a half miles in circumference, and is occupied by five or six traders who have their factories there, and trade with the natives, who bring them India rubber and barwood down the river Muni, immediately opposite Big Eloby, which is occupied altogether by natives, of whom there are perhaps several hundred. We have a station and one Scripture reader there, Eavo by name, a very efficient, earnest man.

"We anchored at Eavo's station about 2 o'clock; and leaving one of the natives to watch the boat, and getting on the back of another (this is the usual way of being landed from boats here, to avoid wetting of our clothes by the surf), I went ashore. Eavo took me to his bamboo house, which is house and church all in one, and belongs to the mission, and gave me a room. I was glad to lie down for a little time on the bed (an oblong frame with nothing but bamboo splits laid on it) and take a rest. It takes but little to weary one in such a climate as this. I cannot tell why it is, but all know by experience that it is so. I had not rested long until I heard the voice of zealous Eavo talking away very earnestly in the next room; and as I after a while peered through where he was, I found him sitting by the table with the gospel of Matthew (in Benga) in his hand, expounding it to a young native with a grave and attentive face on the other side of the table. I went around afterward through six or seven of the towns to see the people and invite them to church, as I intended to preach at night. These towns had a sad and dreary aspect to me, and I scarcely knew why until I smelt the rum on the breath of the men, and then I knew. They live near to the factories, where rum is bartered freely as water, and the poor creatures drink like beasts. May our Father who is merciful forgive the traders this great wrong! Death and sorrow and sin follow in their track; and where the missionaries seek to lure men up to God and heaven, these others, with their cruel snares, gather up scores and hurry them down to hell.

"When night came on, quite a houseful of men and women gathered in to hear the *word*. After preaching six inquirers remained, with whom I spent half an hour or more trying to teach them the way to Christ. They have been inquirers for some time, and seem to have gained some knowledge of the 'way,' but it is hard for minds so dark to gain a clear and saving view of the way to be saved. If the Spirit of God is leading them, they will at last see the light. Nothing is too hard for God to do; he can give sight to all that are blind. I supped before services on a part of my cold chicken and some cakes and a glass of water, which I also carried in my box, for good water is hard to get in many places. After all the duties of the day were done I lay down on my bed of bamboo splits with a shawl under me and one over me, and my carpet-bag under my head for a pillow, and thus slept with tolerable comfort until the morning.

"On Wednesday, 17th, I was up a considerable while before day to be off on my journey. I sat down on the side of my bed and breakfasted on the rest of my chicken by the light of the moon, which was pouring in brightly at the window. After prayer with the men we were again in the boat and away before a nice morning breeze. Eavo went with us to a point on the mainland where his wife was on a visit, and where he wished to talk to the people from the Scriptures.

"We stopped for a moment at Cape St. John, the most northern point of Corisco Bay, to let one of our passengers off. A little farther up the coast we stopped till a canoe came off for the other. About noon we came to Aje, one of the nearest stations on the mainland, about thirty-five miles from Corisco. There is a large native town here at the mouth of the Aje River. The people speak the Benga language with little variation, but they belong to the Bapuku tribe. Many of them stood on the bank as we sailed into the mouth of the river, and hailed our arrival with evident delight. I soon found Makendenga and Ilanga, our Scripture readers at that point, and went with them to the station-house, which was soon crowded with curious faces anxious to hear the news and to see a strange white man. As I was tired and sick with the headache from boating, I laid down and rested for an hour on the bamboo splits. They cooked me a chicken and an egg; most of the chicken I gave to the men, but I drank the soup or broth, which they brought me in a mug. It tasted savory indeed, for I had had no warm drink on my stomach before since I left Corisco. They had neither knife nor fork nor spoon nor salt to give me, though I happened to have all these with me, except the spoon. There was one short wooden spoon in the house, but the men had it busily going round their circle from one to another, dipping, each in his turn, from a pot of food in the centre. The fish and boiled plantains they eat with their fingers, taking all from the same dish. The immense quantity of food that they can dispose of at one time makes me open my eyes with surprise.

"After rest and food I took a short walk around through the wilderness, which is thick all about, to see something of the nature of the coast. I came to the river again a short distance from its mouth, but found it degenerated almost into a stagnant swamp. Mangroves grew plentifully all through it, leaving only here and there an open passage. One peculiarity of the African coast (as Mr. Mackey has sometimes told American audiences) is that the oysters grow on trees. I saw the sight myself, veritable oysters growing on veritable limbs of trees! But it is the tree, not the oyster, that reverses the order of nature; the oyster keeps his place, but the limbs of the tree (mangrove) grow under water. There are immense quantities of oysters growing in this way, not very large, nor of a very good quality, but still having the proper flavor. Mrs. Mackey sometimes uses them at table.

"I was here, too, just in the midst of the elephant region. I did not, however, see any, but the people tell me that the elephants cause them an immense deal of trouble, coming into their farms at night and tearing up and eating their plantains and cassada. Very few elephants, however, are killed in this immediate neighborhood. As

night drew on a goodly number of attentive listeners came in and filled the house, and I preached
to them the story of 'God's wondrous love in giving his Son to die that we might live.' One of the
wives of the headman is an inquirer, and remained
after preaching. I could get but little knowledge
of her thoughts, but I tried to tell her in the
simplest terms the way to God through Christ. It
is a joy to think that, if no more, at least one from
here and there shall at last come up among the
redeemed in glory and help to swell the song of
praise to 'Him that has loved us and washed us in
his blood.' The Scripture readers are simple-
hearted, kind men. It is no hard task to love
them and to feel that they are one with us in
Christ. They hold meetings for prayer morning,
noon and night, reading also the Scriptures and
talking with the people. They keep a school, to
which all may come who will. I had a long
talk with them to encourage them and urge them
on in their good work.

"*Thursday*, 18th.—This morning I was more at
leisure in starting, as we had only a few miles to
sail. So, after prayers and a light breakfast on fish
and eggs, we were away to the beach and in our
boat. Unfortunately we found the anchor fast in

the sand, but a couple of willing fellows jumped
into the water and were soon down to the bottom
to see what was the matter. So by a little effort,
with their assistance, we at last got away. When
we got fairly under way our boat sailed along de-
lightfully before the strong breeze. The next station to which we were going, and the last one, was
at the mouth of the Hanje, another little river
eight or nine miles above the Aje, and among the
Kombe people. Their language also differs but
little from the Benga.

"The Scripture readers here are Jumba and
Etiane, and they are noble fellows, too. We met
them as we went, out on the sea, going to fish with
some other of the natives. They came back with
us in our boat, and their faces showed their joy,
for the arrival of the mission-boat is to them very
much as the arrival of an American ship is to us.
On the beach were numbers of Kombe people gathered, and they followed us into the house. After
I had sat down for a while an old headman came
in, and, after a profound bow and a somewhat cere-
monious welcome, he laid down on the table before
me a paper which he seemed to esteem a most important document. I opened it, and found it to be
the article of agreement between Mr. Mackey and

them for the purchase of the ground on which the station stood.

"I was much pleased with the Kombe people, more, indeed, than with any that I have seen in Africa. They seem generous-hearted, simple-minded, and have not been so spoiled by the corrupting influence of trade. After I had eaten some dinner, which Jumba had been careful to provide (shortly after my arrival he said, 'I go get chicken for you'), I preached for quite a long while to about forty people on the 'parable of the Prodigal Son,' and through the whole of it they were as quiet and attentive an audience as any, I think, I ever stood before. Later in the afternoon, one or two of the young men went with me, and I walked back by a narrow path in the direction of the interior until I came upon the river again. Here I found nearly all of the women of the town busily engaged in building dams across the stream to catch fish. They build two dams near together, and then bail out the water between them. In this way they sometimes catch quantities of fish, chiefly catfish. When I left them I bade them good-bye and wished them success in catching plenty of fish. They said, 'Bless us, that we may catch plenty of fish,' and the words sent a chill through me as I thought that in their blindness they would put man in the place of his Maker. I pointed them to Him who alone has power to bless and prosper in every station and duty of life. They said 'Yes, all the people in Hanje know that your God is a very great God.' But it is a difficult matter to make them believe and feel that the 'white man's God' is their God also. I urged them to come in to hear about God at night, but they said they would be too tired to walk so far, and were going to sleep on the bank of the river.

"As I returned to Hanje by another path I suddenly came upon traces of elephants, and they were so recent that it startled me for a moment when I thought that I was then standing in the tracks that wild elephants had made not long before. As I passed along I came on more frequent traces, which seemed to make it evident that elephants were abundant there and would not be difficult to find. Late in the afternoon I went with the Scripture readers to examine a house, in a town a short distance up the river, which they wished to hire for mission purposes. We got into a canoe and paddled up the narrow, deep stream. In some places it was so thickly covered with mangroves as scarcely to leave a passage for the canoe. It was a quiet, solemn ride, because of the dreariness of the mangroves about and overhead. At length we landed in a grove of palms, about twenty in number, and as tall and beautiful as I have ever seen. They stood in rows as though they had been planted, and their branches met at the top and made a deep, quiet shade underneath. They stood there like majestic old columns, grand and beautiful; and since I was in Westminster or St. Paul's I have not been in a place where I felt such awe, and where there seemed to be such a deep, solemn quiet, as though it were a temple of the living God.

"After we had examined the house I went back and preached to a good audience at Hanje in the evening, and conversed with the mother and sister of Jumba after preaching.

"*Friday*, August 19.—This morning we were all up by daylight, and, after prayers, got off. Our own boat was anchored out from shore nearly half a mile, because of the rocks near the land, so we went off to it in Jumba's boat. I bade good-bye to Jumba, as noble a Christian, I think, as I have ever seen; everything about him seems tempered with the spirit of the gospel. His face shines with that peculiar lustre which speaks so plainly of happiness and peace within. At another time I hope to give you some account of him, as his history is interesting. When we got our sails spread I took a little breakfast, viz., some biscuit, hot fish, and a glass of water. The fish are cooked by wrapping them with pepper in plantain leaves (green), and thus laying them on the coals. My breakfast had to serve me till night, as we landed nowhere and I could eat nothing while we were sailing. The trip up the coast is pleasant enough, but going back it is very tedious, as the winds are all against us, and we are compelled to tack back and forward all the time. Thus, as we were now on our return, we were sailing back and forth all day, and making but little progress. In the afternoon a man and a boy came off to us from the shore in a canoe. He brought twenty-seven ears of dried corn, a chicken, and some dried fish. I bought them all for about eight cents. We buy almost everything that the natives bring us, as we generally find use for it at the mission.

"About night I was glad to find that we were drawing near to Cape St. John, where we expected to stay all night, and where I wished to preach. When we got there, however, I was obliged to put off the preaching, as there was such a hubbub on our arrival (about 7½ o'clock), and as the men were tired and hungry, and I myself was tired and had eaten nothing since daylight. When we got into a hut I stretched myself out on the 'bamboo splits' to rest, while the boatmen and the people from the town, who had gathered in, kept up a terrible talking. If any natives are near there is no quiet, for they are incessant talkers and talk almost at the top of their voices; their nearness to the sea gives them, I suppose, the habit of loud talking.

"At 9 o'clock the women brought in some fish and boiled plantains for the men, and in an almost incredibly short time they had cut up my chicken and boiled it in a pot, and now I had it smoking before me. The legs and wings and neck tasted very savory and tender, and on these I made my supper and gave the rest to the men. They found me a place to sleep—a little hut which was new and nice enough, but only about ten feet square, and with no hole in it for ventilation or for the escape of smoke but the door. It was used for parlor, bed-room and kitchen. As it was a warm night, and the fire left burning in the middle of the floor, and as I must of necessity shut the door to keep out thieves, I could scarcely imagine what would be the result by morning. But no other house could be found, so I had the fire put out, and, shutting my door, I laid down and slept pretty well until morning. When I opened my door again at daylight, I saw an old man moving about near by, and from him I got some water to wash my face, which refreshed me as much as my sleep.

"*Saturday*, August 20.—As I could not preach last night, I got the people together this morning about 8 o'clock and preached to them, and had a solemn and, I hope, profitable meeting. Soon we got started again on our way to Little Eloby, where I expected to spend the Sabbath and preach to the traders. We were obliged to row out a considerable distance from the point so as to catch the wind, but the tide was against us and also the wind. After rowing a considerable distance with great difficulty, and after breaking one oar, the men asked me to let them put in to shore and wait for a change of tide, which I thought it better to do. When we landed I saw a little town on the hill above the beach. So, putting a couple of bananas and as many biscuits in my pocket to breakfast on by the way, I took the interpreter and went up to preach to the people. When we got there we found all the people away but one woman, but small as my congregation was I did not fail to preach the gospel to her in as plain and simple a way as I could. She said Mr. Clemens had preached to them once, but she did not remember what he had told them.

"After change of tide we started again, and this time got under way, though with some difficulty, and in a little while again a calm fell on us, so that it was late in the afternoon before we got under full sail for Eloby. I was not a little glad, however, when, about 8 o'clock at night, we landed at Eloby and I found my way to Mr. Watson's house, and there enjoyed again some of the 'white man's' cleanliness and comfort. He immediately sent his boys to get me some coffee and ham and eggs, which I relished after my cold food, and especially as I had eaten nothing that day except my biscuits and bananas in the morning.

"The five or six traders settled on this little island (about a mile and a half in circumference) live very comfortably in bachelor style, as there are no white ladies in this part of Africa except missionary ladies. They have good houses and plenty of goods which they exchange with the natives for India-rubber, bass-wood, ivory, etc., as

they bring these to them from the mainland. I
was acquainted with the other traders on the island,
and they came in to see me shortly after I arrived
at Mr. Watson's.

"*Sabbath*, August 21.—This morning before I
got up I heard Mr. Watson calling to me that the
mail had at last come—the mail for which we had
been looking for the last twenty days. My letters
were among the rest, for I had left directions to
have them sent to Eloby to meet me, if the mail
should come while I was gone. I had quite a
package—two mails in one. I read my home
letters and another one, but the rest I put aside
until Monday. I spent a tolerably quiet and
pleasant Sabbath here; the traders met and I
preached to them as plainly and pointedly as I
could. They were apparently very glad to have
services, and when preaching was over one of them
passed a hat around and took up a collection for
the mission. They handed me five dollars in silver; I suppose each man gave a dollar.

"*Monday*, August 22.—Started early from Eloby
this morning and reached Corisco about noon. It
is much more comfortable on land than tossing
about on the sea; but we are not to study comfort
when all Africa is dying for the lack of light.

" *Thursday*, September 1.—To-day our mail for September came, and although I had scarcely digested all the good news I had received a few days before, yet I gave it a hearty welcome. We learn by this mail that our supplies and reinforcements will be likely to reach us by the last of the month. It will be a great day when a ship from America lands at Corisco and brings more missionaries. Dr. Nassau is very busy fixing up everything about his premises to receive his wife. I am busy rebuilding the boat-house and reroofing part of the dwelling-house, and attending to everything that is to be done before the rains commence, which will be about the 15th of this month. Will also have to take an inventory of all the mission property, so as to make report to the Board at the end of the year, and also to put in order the store-house to receive the new supplies.

" *Saturday*, September 3.—Spent part of this day dressing up and cleaning out our little grave-yard, so that it might not seem overgrown and neglected when Mr. de Heer comes—his wife lies buried there.

" *Sabbath*, 4th.—Preached at Alongo. Had a good turn-out, about forty-four in number, and among them two or three old headmen. At night I con-

ducted the services for Dr. Nassau at Evangasimba.
It was monthly concert. We have monthly concert and take a collection on the first Sabbath of
every month.

"Our heavenly Father has kept me thus far in
remarkably good health, much better, indeed, than
is common for new-comers, however I dare not
boast, but should be humble and thankful.

"I could scarcely venture so long a letter as this
for any place but home, lest it would seem a wearisome task to read it; but I can trust that you will
not grow weary of it, unless by some means I have
failed to make it interesting. I shall not always
write you at so great length, but as long as I live
and my parents live I hope to write regularly,
and at some length, too, if by this means I can
afford any gratification to them. This is probably
the only means left me, or the only way that I
shall ever have of contributing to their enjoyment
or comfort. And whatever time I may spend in
this way I shall look upon as time well and accept-
ably spent.

"We are looking for Mr. de Heer, Mrs.
Clemens and Mrs. Nassau about the last of this
month; we have heard from them and of their
arrival on the coast, a good piece north, about Li-

beria. It will be a very busy time when the vessel reaches here. There are many of my friends to whom I would be glad to write, but I find if I carry on a large correspondence, it will consume a great amount of my time which I cannot conscientiously spare from my work here. I have never been able to get a letter off to my old friends at Morrison, Illinois, until this mail. It was a shame to neglect any who have been so kind to me for so long a time, but it seemed unavoidable.

" *August* 23.—Conducted the prayer-meeting at Evangasimba; spoke to the people on the healing of blind Bartimeus. Gave out the hymn, ' Awake, and sing the song of Moses and the Lamb.' While waiting for Mrs. Mackey to raise the tune, my ears were surprised to hear some sweet strains coming from another quarter of the house. It was from the little girls of the school—about twenty in number, and most of them from ten to fourteen years of age. They had commenced to the tune of ' There'll be no more sorrow there,' and with their soft young voices they made music so sweet that my heart was melted almost to tears. In the darkness of a heathen land, to hear the praise of Jesus sung so sweetly makes one dream of heaven.

"*August* 29.—Preached yesterday at Alongo on

'Turn ye, turn ye, for why will ye die?' Not a very large congregation. Preached in the afternoon at Ngume's town, on 'Whosoever will, let him take of the water of life freely.' Fever took hold of me slightly in the afternoon, probably the effects of my Kombe trip. The fever is also on me to-day, with headache and a sore eye. Last night I was restless. Have set the men at the boat-house this morning to repair it.

"*September* 16.—Recovered to-day from my fourth attack of fever. All have been light, lasting only a few days at most, and only producing a feeling of inexpressible worthlessness."

In a letter dated Corisco, October 5, 1864, to his brother James, Mr. Paull writes: " The friendship of any that have been my true friends I find has not grown weaker by my being so far away ; nor do I believe it ever will. But even if it did, this much I know—that I could still be happy here in my work, and in the comforts God can and does bestow, were I assured that I had not a friend on earth. They greatly mistake who think it a dry and dreary life to be a Christian. If it is dry and dreary to be full of peace, to be perfectly contented and happy wherever God places you or with whatever he sends you, to be ready for either life or death, rather indeed preferring to die than to live, then it is dry and dreary to be a Christian. If you are not one yet, Jim, this will be like holding up a beautiful flower and discussing its form and varied colors to a blind boy; you will neither see nor appreciate what I have said. You think your pleasures now are delightful; so does every one of your age; but when you become a Christian you will wish that you had let them go to the wind, and that you had sought with all your heart the joy which is so much purer. Begin to look heavenward with all your heart; be in earnest."

To his parents:

"EVANGASIMBA STATION, October 20, 1864.

"This morning we got our mail away to Gaboon, and I am determined not to delay my letter-writing so long. I would like to make my letters for home a record of current events. The pressure of business is over, and I am beginning to think of getting ready for my monthly trip to the stations on the mainland, and also of taking up again in earnest the study of the Benga.

"I saddled Charley this afternoon, and took a ride to Alongo to see how Mr. and Mrs. De Heer were getting on in their new home. As I rode along the white and glistening beach I saw a fine picture of African life. Just by a cluster of cocoanut trees a batch of people were lounging on the sand, half in the sun and half in the shade. Some one had exerted himself and pulled some cocoanuts, so the rest and he together were enjoying the fruit of his labor. They seemed to be happy as kings as they lounged on the sand, drinking the rich milk that the cocoanut gives without labor or price. One cocoanut was left as I rode among them, which they gave me, tearing off the thick outer husk so that I could easily get at the milk. After drinking my draught, and promising the boy who gave it some pay when he came to Evangasimba, I rode on to Mr. De Heer's.

"*Monday*, October 24.—Yesterday was my day to preach at Gobi. On my way I saw what the Psalmist meant when he spoke of 'the dark places of the earth being full of the habitations of cruelty,' and also I understood better the thought that was in Paul's mind when he spoke of the heathen as being 'past feeling.' A little fellow about ten years old was lying on the sand of the beach crying with all his might. Three almost grown men had hold of his arms and legs and were scraping and scouring him (for he was almost covered with

sand) with pieces of bamboo as you would a pig.
The fellows left off their work as I came up and
commenced to explain that he was sick, and this
was their manner of cure; and I suppose this is
the usual way of curing such diseases, but it makes
one's blood run cold to think of its cruelty. The
little fellow was covered with scabs and sores, and
these they scraped with their sticks and sand until
blood was coming from every sore; then they sent
him with his fresh and bleeding wounds to wash
in the salt sea. My heart bled for the little fellow,
but the chief work was done when I got there.
They seem to have no tenderness of feeling, no
sympathy with suffering; their hearts seem to be
blunted by sin until they are hard as a rock.
These skin diseases are remarkably common
among the people, and are among the most
pitiful and sickening sights that one meets with.
I suppose they are brought on by their abomi-
nable lives. Some of them live like beasts, and
are besotted with almost every crime. Sometimes
I have seen their noses eaten away, their bodies
and limbs shriveled up at times. Often I see
great and incurable ulcers in different parts of
the body, and a sort of leprosy is common among
them which makes their appearance loathsome.

Hundreds of years yet to come may not do away with these terrible sights. Little by little, as they learn to know the great Physician and seek his balm to heal the heart, many of their bodily ills will pass away, for a pure heart will make a holy life, and it is their impure life that brings their diseases.

"Men at home do not know anything of Africa's sorrows. Poor people! the heart that sees them can pity, but they need more than pity. Strong hands and kind hearts are needed—they are needed here by the score—who will point them to better things and help them to rise up and enjoy them. America, looking back from this land, gives one a peculiar feeling. It is impossible to convince one's self that ministers or Christians there do one tithe of what they ought to for this wretched people. The land at home seems full of ministers, who crowd and jostle each other to get a little flock to whom they may give the bread of life, but they forget to turn and look for a moment this way, where mighty hosts of these miserable people are starving to death for lack of this very bread which they could so easily spare.

"*Thursday*, October 27.—This is one of Africa's most beautiful mornings. The thermometer stands between 75° and 80°, and the dryness of the air has been moistened and cooled by last night's rain. It is such mornings as these that make one think Corisco almost a paradise. The plantains all around with their great leaves wave and rustle in the breeze, and the orange trees begin to give forth a fragrant smell, for they are just now laden with delicate white blossoms and with the new growth of buds and leaves, and the lemon trees are full of rich green fruit, just a little more than formed. The wild flowers, too, are springing all around, and every footpath is made beautiful with them. Over the tree-tops clamber thousands of vines bearing a rich burden of beautiful bell-shaped flowers; and the great African lilies are putting out here and there in two or three different varieties. Indeed everything, since the rains are coming, is beginning to look beautiful and bright, and the air is almost enchanting, just warm enough to be pleasant, and kept fresh by a constant breeze from the sea. If anything else is needed to add to the pleasantness of this African home, then we have it in the songs of the birds which throng every bush and tree in hosts almost innumerable, and warble forth their constant songs sweeter and richer, I think, than any I have ever heard before.

"The wife of my old friend Nqume came this morning carrying a chicken and a bunch of plantains, but she would not sell them to Mrs. Mackey. She said Nqume had sent them as a *dash* (a present) to 'Pauloo.' It is usually very nice to receive presents, but the case is somewhat different among this people: they think that every good turn deserves another and a far better. If they give you a little thing they expect a big one in return. So as Nqume's wife went away she very quietly took hold of her cloth or dress, and pointing to it said that it was all she had, intimating that a new dress would be a very acceptable present. So I suppose I shall have to give her one. I gave Nqume a cloth some time ago, and he immediately suggested that he would like to have some tobacco, and not long after he modestly hinted that he ought to have a new hat also.

"The people need but little clothing; the usual dress of both men and women is simply a piece of cotton cloth or calico wrapped about them. This, with a string of beads and an old hat, if they can get one (though they are usually bareheaded), completes the outfit. Some are beginning to wear shirts, which are made up by the girls in the mission, and some of those who have been under

the instruction of the mission wear coat and pants.
If one of the old headmen gets a present of a coat
or hat he will wear it on particular occasions, but
not ordinarily.

"As I rode up to Gobi last Sabbath I met old
Peter, the oldest headman, perhaps, on the island,
and the one who was heir to the throne when the
last king died, but he refused the honor. Peter
is a little round-headed, funny-looking man, and
when I met him he was dressed in his Sunday
suit, which made him look all the more odd. He
had a big silk hat, a little worse for the wear and
somewhat dinged, a tremendous large coat made of
heavy cloth and reaching to his knees, looked like
an overcoat, and this he had buttoned. Thus he
trudged along thinking himself finely dressed,
though he was barefooted and barelegged to the
knees.

" *November* 1.—I would have been away to-day
on my trip to the mainland, but concluded to wait
another day for the mail. We saw the French
steamer on her way to Gaboon. We are all anxious
to get our letters.

"I received by the last mail a note from Dr.
Plumer. He says, 'I forewarned you, I believe,
that your correspondence would fail to come up to

13

time. Jehovah Jireh'—the Lord will provide. So I find it—the Lord provides: and I would not fear any lack of happiness, come what might.

"Lizzie in her long letter of July 26 gives me an account of the celebration of the 4th, and very vividly the whole picture comes up before me. I remember everything about home with strange distinctness. Every hill and valley, every farm and field, every tree and shrub and rivulet stands out so clearly in my mind that I seem to walk among them again. The features of every face are clear, and every voice sounds distinctly, so that I seem to be walking and talking among you as of old. It seems but a step home again, and I often pass through the front gate and up the yard, and into the house, and through every room and out again into the orchard or through the fields. All this gives me pleasure, but I am not unhappy when I come to myself and find that my home is here. On the contrary, my happiness is truer and purer here, at my sacred work in this dark land, than ever it has been in my life before. If God takes away some comforts, he well knows how to replace them with others which are fourfold richer and better. It is a good God that we serve; all the treasures of his storehouse are thrown open to us when we draw near to him. Honey is not sweeter than is the love of Christ, when we keep near to him and constrain him by our importunity to abide with us.

"My privations have not been very great, nor have I been called on to make sacrifices such as many other missionaries have made—at least not such sacrifices as the world will ever know of—but such as they are, already it seems to me according to the promise, a 'hundred-fold' has been returned in spiritual blessings; and the promise of 'life everlasting' with its infinite fullness is yet to be made good. Happy are we whose God is the Lord. People of the world who know nothing of the love of Christ think us fools for rejoicing in him, but I think I can say that I am perfectly willing to be called a fool for his sake. It is no hazardous venture when we stake everything for time and eternity on the love and faithfulness of Christ; but we only know this when we have made the venture.

"I am glad to learn that father's health is so much better and that everything about home is so prosperous and cheering. It was one of our gloomy forebodings when I thought of becoming a missionary that his health might fail, and when I would be

most needed at home I would be far away among
the heathen. But divine faithfulness crowns every
step in the path of duty with blessings; his health,
instead of failing, has only grown better, and we
will pray that it may still continue to do so. I am
sorry to know that Mr. Burnet (pastor at C.) is so
feeble as to walk on crutches. He has often been
in my mind, and I trust I have sometimes been in
his prayers. It is pleasant to hope that the Christians about home, for whom I have a warmer
regard than ever, sometimes remember me when
they pray. Aunt E.'s troubles are very sore. I
suppose she is weighed down with sorrow and can
hardly read aright the lesson that God is teaching
her—'Whom the Lord loveth he chasteneth.' If
this is the way we are permitted to look at our
sorrows, then the burden becomes light, and we are
tempted to say, 'If by our sorrows we may know
that thou dost love us, then, O Lord, let them
come!'

"Our mail came this evening, bringing a good
long letter from mother, which was full of satisfaction, as her letters always are. As a correspondent
I fear that none of us, her children, will ever equal
her. A short letter also came from Mr. Mackey,
and it gave us no little joy to know that he is now

on his way back to Corisco, and will doubtless be here by the next mail. This will free me from the secular work, and then I will be a missionary. I had a letter from Rev. W. Thompson, in Glasgow, telling me that he expects to bring a wife out with him to Calabar. I met the lady in Scotland. African life will be a change for her, as she lived in splendid style, with every comfort that she could desire, in Glasgow. Since my letters have come, I start on my trip to-morrow morning to visit the stations on the mainland.

" *November* 2.—Started to-day for Kombe and Benita; reached Iloby and stayed over night.

" *November* 3.—Reached Aje and spent the night; preached to a full house.

" *November* 4.—Reached Hanje and spent the night.

" *November* 5.—Reached Benita—preached.

" *November* 6.—Preached in three towns at Benita—placed Mbata there. Everything promising.

" *November* 9.—Reached home to-night. Landed on the east side and took tea with Mrs. De Heer.

" *November* 19.—I have not written since my return from the mainland, and I will not say anything of the trip now. I am very well; surely I

never was in better health.   Dr. Nassau remarked
to-night that I looked younger than when I came.
I visited Mr. De Heer the other day to give them
some account of my mainland trip.   They are
greatly interested in the mainland work, and expect to go there when Mr. Clark comes.   My own
opinion and the opinion of the rest of the missionaries is, that the mainland is just as healthy as
Corisco.   The traders that live on the coast have
just as good health as we.   There is a mighty and
a noble work to do here; other generations for
hundreds of years to come may find an outlet to
their zeal here, and I pray that the zeal in each
coming generation may be a thousand-fold greater
than it is now.   If Christ is to get his inheritance
among the heathen soon, then Christian parents
must begin to teach their children to love missions
at home around the fireside: there is where missionaries grow.   If the claims of the heathen and
their deep wretchedness become a common topic
around every Christian fireside, and if constant
prayer also is made to God for them, then the next
generation will see multitudes of earnest hearts
hastening to heathen shores, where there is now
but a lone traveler.

"*November* 20.—I write a few lines to close my

letter to-night and give you the latest possible word. We have just come in from evening services at the church, which is at one end of our yard. We have been greatly troubled with thieves of late stealing chickens and plantains. Mrs. Mackey came out of church this evening for a moment and saw a fellow passing along in the dark by the house. We found his tracks when we came home, but that will not amount to much without the thief. We have the house and grounds all surrounded with a fence of sharp and strong pickets, but still they get in. They almost think it no harm to steal, particularly from white people; for they think their goods and property come to them for nothing.

"Our ears have been stunned this evening, and indeed for several days, by a great drumming and noise at a town near by. The headman of the town is sick, and the people are trying to drive away the evil spirit that has made him sick. They dance and halloo and beat their drums, and make the sick man dance as long as he is able. This is a part of their medicine for sick people. I went to Gobi to-day to preach. As it rained nearly all day I scarcely expected anybody out, but I was surprised and glad to find twenty-five or thirty there from the towns."

"November, 1864.

"I promised to send you some little sketch of my last trip to the mainland. Perhaps it may be of some interest, or at least entertain you a little; and if it does this it is well, for this is almost the only possible way left me of contributing to your enjoyment. Making these trips every month or six weeks is now my regular business; and I really like the work better than anything else. It is missionary work, preaching the gospel to those who have never heard it, talking to inquirers, and trying to help and encourage the scattered Christians that I find. This trip was partly with the design of establishing a new station up the coast somewhere, which I did at the mouth of the Benita River, about fifty miles north from here.

" I started November 2, after getting the Gaboon mail-boat away, which had brought our letters the night before. Mrs. Mackey packed me a box of provisions, a more plentiful supply than I had the last time; and it shall be even more plentiful the next time, for I find that every comfort is just so much of a saving to the health. Mrs. Mackey, who is a willing and abundant provider, put up coffee and sugar and tea and a little pot to make them in. I had greatly missed the warm drink on the last trip, doing without it nearly a week. I had also a supply of beef and ham and bread ; the eggs and chickens that I needed were easy to get on the way. Mrs. Clemens added to my stock a little jar of jelly and one of maple molasses, and they proved a most valuable addition. A couple of shawls and a pillow I took for sleeping on, an overcoat also and umbrella for protection against the rain, and a change of clean linen. In a box I stowed knives and cloth and shirts and fish-hooks, etc., for buying food for the men, and whatever the natives on the way might wish to sell.

"With five boatmen, and Andike for an interpreter, and several passengers who asked to go along to see friends on the mainland, we got away about ten o'clock in the morning. This time I escaped seasickness and felt tolerably comfortable all the way. Andike had with him a bundle of hot *conchs* or shell fish which his wife had cooked for him, and of which the people are very fond. He handed some of them to me, of which I ate one or two (they are as large as an oyster), and found them rich as butter. They are a great article of food with the people. At every low tide you see hundreds of women out in search of them. About 3 o'clock we reached Large Eloby, where we have a station, but I only stopped a few moments, expecting to return that way.

"Having the mission accounts to settle with the traders on Little Eloby, I went on there and spent the night. After breakfast on Thursday, 3d, I got off to Aje, my next stopping-place. One of our passengers was the wife of Imunga, the brother of the king on Corisco, but virtually the king himself. To give you an idea of queenly attire in Africa, I will describe her dress. Her hair was platted up in a heavy, greasy roll on the top of her head, and on this rested an old hat (man's hat), made secure to the hair with an iron pin six or eight inches long. Around her neck were some strings of beads. On her ankles and wrists were, I think, just one hundred and forty brass and copper rings. Besides these she wore a large cloth such as I have before described. This was her complete attire.

"About 3 o'clock we reached Aje, and anchored in the mouth of the little river. I went to our mission-house, where Mackendenga and Ilanga, the Scripture readers, live. After taking a rest, they got ready something for the men and myself to eat. They seem to understand that a chicken is almost the only part of native food that a white man relishes, so they immediately suggest one and get it ready. Their plan of cooking is simply to boil in an iron pot until thoroughly cooked, and then season with cayenne pepper, which grows abundantly here. They bring the chicken on a plate and the broth in the bowl. The broth would be delicious and savory if it were not so terribly hot with pepper. The men usually eat at the same little tables with me. They have a wash-basin full of *unguesa* (sliced cassada), which looks like cold sliced potatoes. They dip their fingers into the dish, and eat this along with some hot fish and a part of my chicken, which they never refuse.

" It is a strange custom these people have—whenever you sit down to eat every one else not eating immediately goes out of the house and stays away until you are done. There is a natural dislike among them to have any one see them eat. Another thing I notice, and I believe it is a universal custom in Africa, they never eat a morsel of food without taking some water afterward and washing their mouths. They all have good and beautiful teeth, too, so the one seems to be, partly at least, the consequence of the other. I heard great complaints here about the elephants coming into their farms and destroying their plantains, and they do not know how to cope with so immense an enemy.

"In the evening the bell was rung (a large dinner bell), and Mackendenga lighted the long roll of resin, which burns like our rosin and is the chief native light (there is a tree here which yields it abundantly), and the people began to gather for service. Soon all the seats were full and still the people came; benches were brought in and they were all filled, until there was room for no more in the house. Then the people gathered about the door and in the little yard in front of the house until all available space was occupied. So I preached to them as they sat crowded together in the dim light, and as they stood about the door waiting to hear. I do not know that I ever had better attention than from these dusky children of sorrow, with minds even darker than their skins, as I opened the news to them of a fountain for sin and uncleanness, for sorrow and every human woe, and invited them to come and drink freely without money. I had a fine interpreter, and preached with great comfort and interest on my whole trip, for there is no work that I enjoy like preaching the gospel to the poor. My old interpreter I have exchanged for another (Andike); you will see his name in the Foreign Missionary, often, as a licentiate and elder of the Church. He interprets with great fluency, and has a better knowledge of the English than almost any other native.

"*Friday*, 4th.—Eight o'clock I got away for Hanje. I could find no hot water to make coffee, so I breakfasted on boiled duck eggs and soda crackers, with a little of Mrs. Clemens' maple syrup. At prayers, before starting, I had a full house again. I read and explained the Scriptures. The wife of the headman at this place hopes she is a Christian, and wishes to unite with the church.

"About noon we reached Hanje, where Jumba and Etiane are the Scripture readers. We were obliged to anchor out from the shore on account of rocks, and a canoe came off for us. When we went ashore a crowd of people followed to the mission-house to sit and hear the news, for they have nothing to do but sit about all day, and wherever there is the least excitement they speedily follow it. After a while they brought in native baskets and wooden spoons and melanga to sell, some of which I bought. When we went in I saw that Jumba had a chicken tied by the leg in one corner of the house; this he soon carried out and cooked for dinner. Here I at last got some hot water to make coffee, and this I relished, for boating is terribly hard work on the stomach, and some warm drink saves much discomfort. I could scarcely call my mixture coffee, though it tasted like excellent coffee to me. It was hot water poured on some ground coffee. This, after it had stood a few minutes, I poured out and sweetened and drank without cream.

"I spent an hour or two after dinner up in that beautiful and solemn palm grove I spoke of on my other trip. Jumba paddled me up in a canoe. At the foot of one of the tall trees I found four or five men lying, and, looking up, I saw another in the top of the tree gathering palm wine. They tap the tree in the top and then fasten a great jug there, into which the wine runs. Every day or so some one goes up and dips out the wine, when it is brought down and divided. It is almost of a milk-white appearance, and will intoxicate after it becomes a little old. The natives drink great quantities of it, but I believe that the rum which the traders bring to the coast is fast taking its place; death and destruction the traders are scattering in their path.

"After a good sleep and a comfortable breakfast and prayers, we got away Saturday, 5th, for the

Benita River. We had to go out to the boat in a canoe, and these are uncomfortable to ride in, being like an egg-shell, and a trifle will topple them over. Just as I got in the canoe a breaker struck it and tumbled me over, but I fell inside and not in the water. After we got part way up the coast to Benita a man paddled out to us in a canoe, who had with him a little boy that had never seen a white man before, and he evidently thought me a strange being, for he began to cry and seemed to beg his father to take him away as quickly as possible. The man had never heard of God, nor of Christ, and as I had the Gospel of John, in Benga, lying near by me I read to him, 'God so loved the world that he gave,' etc., and explained the way of salvation, hoping that the truth might not only sink into his own mind, but that he might also bear it back to his people.

"At last we came in sight of the Benita, a broad and beautiful river—two or three miles wide, I judge, at the mouth. On the south side of it are several factories. I landed for an hour at one of them. The agent there I knew, and he is quite a genteel young Scotchman. He had been to Corisco to consult Dr. Nassau about his health. From there I sailed across the mouth of the river into a beautiful little bay where I thought of establishing a station, and leaving Mbata, whom I had taken along.

"While we were getting ready to land, men, women and children to the number of thirty, perhaps, gathered on the beach from the towns near by. When I landed among them they gave me a friendly welcome, shaking me by the hand and looking quite pleased. With the aid of Andike, I made them a little speech, telling them that I had come to stay a little while among them, and that perhaps I would leave them a missionary to teach them of God, etc., if they were willing. I then asked them if they could give me a house to live in while I stayed, but they did not wait to reply: off they started to the nearest town, which meant that I was to follow. Eight or ten men were in front, I came next, and after me the boatmen with the baggage, then the women and children behind. They never stopped till they came to the house of the headman, and into it the whole procession went, boxes and all, and as many more people as were able crowded in along with the others. I then made them another little speech, explaining more fully why I had come and what we wished to do.

"At night the people came again, filling the house to overflowing, and I preached to them as plainly and simply as I could the 'Story of the cross,' which they never before had heard. How they listened! I surely never before had better attention than I had there from these children of the night. There is a peculiar, indescribable joy in preaching the gospel to the benighted. I never was engaged in happier work; nor do I know that I ever was happier than as I lay down that night in a little cheerless bamboo hut, all alone, and feeling that I was surely a stranger in a very strange land. It is a peculiar sensation that sometimes comes over me when out on these trips, though it is not unpleasant—I mean a sense of aloneness in the great, wide world—a feeling that I have no longer any place that can really be called home; no place where there will be any warm heart-welcomes awaiting my return, and so the consequence is that I am happy and at home anywhere wherever the blue sky bends above me, whether it be on the sea or alone in the smoky hut of the Kombes.

"November 6 was the Sabbath, which I intended to spend among the people where I stopped. In the morning the rain was pouring down in

14

torrents, and so continued most of the day. I got up from my bed of bamboo slats, on which I had a comfortable sleep, and Tom (as he said the white men called him), my host, brought me some water to wash. After I had eaten my breakfast of coffee, eggs, sardines and bread—the latter I shared with Tom, for he said 'I like white man's bread *too much*'—I went into the headman's house about 10 o'clock to preach to the people. Soon they gathered and crowded the house, while I preached to them from Acts, on the 'Unknown God.' A more attentive audience I think I never saw, listening with a fixed gaze through the whole discourse. At 2 o'clock I preached in another town, and in the evening in a third. In all these was the same good attention.

"As I got wet in the afternoon, going from one town to another, I stepped into the house next to the one I occupied to dry my feet by the fire. I found a little girl here, the betrothed wife of Tom, though she was only eight or nine years old. Tom had promised to send her down with me to Corisco to school; but the moment she saw me she set up a terrible crying, enough to alarm the whole town. I do not know that she had ever seen a white man before. She was still full of tears on Monday morning, and on this account I left her till I should be ready to go back again. As I sat in my house I saw a man working away on his new house just across the narrow street. As Tom was standing near him I said, 'Tom, don't you know this is Sunday?' 'Yes,' said he, 'I done tell him so.' I do not know that the workman knew anything about Sunday or that he had ever heard of it before, but Tom had lived among white men and learned something of the Sabbath.

"*Monday*, November 7.—The headmen came together early to get some little present before I went away; this they always expect. I left Mbata in their care, charging them to treat him kindly, and telling them that if they did so, and attended well on his instructions, that we would probably build a mission-house among them. They were to give him one of their houses to live in for a few months, and after that we expect to build one for him. I got away about 8 o'clock on my return to Corisco, nearly the whole town following me down to the beach to bid me good-bye, and I feeling rather sorry to part with them, as my short stay had been so pleasant and had impressed me so favorably with them. The sea was smooth as glass as we sailed away, and the sky clear and beautiful. No

May morning in America was ever more lovely. As I looked up the broad river I had a fine view of the grand old mountains that run along the coast about forty miles back from the sea. There seem to be two or three ranges running parallel with each other, and just as bold and lofty as our mountains in Pennsylvania.

"I hope the time is not far away when we shall be able to carry the work back among these ranges, and even behind them. Here is where the Fan tribe lives, the cannibals of whom Du Chaillu speaks in his work; but they are a bold and thrifty people, and perhaps the gospel would take a deeper hold on them than on the more effeminate tribes nearer the sea. About noon we reached Hanje again, not intending, however, to stop, but an old headman came off to the boat with complaints against one of the Scripture readers, and his business was to have me go ashore and 'talk the palaver.' This is the native way of settling a trouble—calling all the people in town together and talking the matter over. This they call 'settling the palaver.'

"I went ashore, and after the old man had collected the people in a large bamboo house he arose and made a speech stating all his grievances. I made them another one or two, trying to arrange the matter as satisfactorily as possible, and finally they declared the 'palaver settled.' This consumed a good deal more time than I have occupied in telling of it, for the discussion lasted long, and part of the time ran high among themselves, and then it was like being in 'bedlam.' Every one would jump to his feet, gesticulating fearfully, running toward each other and shouting at the tops of their voices, giving also at the same time a significant shake of the forefinger in each other's faces.

"We hurried on to Aje to spend the night, but the wind fell and the men had to take to their oars, so that we did not reach it till 9 o'clock at night. Every one was in bed, but Mackendenga heard the songs of the boatmen, as they usually sing some plaintive strain when they row (all their music, indeed, is of a somewhat mournful character), and came down to welcome us. I got a good night's rest here, and indeed I had begun to feel the need of it pretty badly.

"*November* 8.—I was awake at daylight, and the people came around the house with mats and ducks and chickens to sell, some of which I bought and brought to Corisco, for it is beginning to be difficult to get as much fresh food as we need. We landed again at a town two or three miles farther down the coast, where I expected to get a boy or two for the school. Evaha was the headman, and a pleasant, kind old man I found him to be. His son, a very nice boy, was to come with me, but had a sore foot, and I left him till another trip. As neither the men nor I had any warm food in the morning, we stopped long enough to have breakfast. I bought a very big fish and had it cooked with some plantains for them, and Evaha had a chicken cooked for me, which tasted savory, for my appetite had become strong by this time. Evaha made me a present of a bunch of plantains and divided his large cake of udika with me, because he saw that I liked it with my chicken. Udika is made of oily nuts pounded together and hardened into a large cake; this they shave down with a knife and use it for thickening the chicken gravy.

"I hoped that possibly we might reach Corisco to-day, but the wind was bad, and, after a whole day's sailing, we only reached Cape St. John in the night — twenty miles from Corisco. I had given up my intention of returning by Eloby, as the return thus far had been so tedious and wearisome, on account of bad winds, that I felt anxious to get home as soon as possible.

"After a tolerably good night's sleep at Cape St. John, we left in the morning in the midst of the rain for Corisco. We had not got far out to sea when one of the principal ropes broke and fell through the pulley at the top of the mast. This rendered our sail useless. One of the boys climbed the mast to put the rope through the pulley again, but just as he was doing it a wave struck the boat and the mast cracked, and the boy had to come down. We then pulled back to shore into still water, and fixed the rope securely and got fairly under way again. We reached Corisco in the evening. I got out at the north side of the island (Alongo) and took tea with Mr. and Mrs. de Heer. They gave me a hearty, homelike welcome. The boys took the boat on to Evangasimba, and I walked down after night. I was gone a little over a week, and, after so much tossing on the waves in an open boat, I found the quiet and comfort of Evangasimba grateful enough. There is much that is wearisome about the mainland journeys, but it is the work that I like, and it is a field that promises to yield fruit if there is faithful sowing."

In a letter to his mother and sister, dated Evangasimba, November 22, 1864, Mr. Paull writes:

"It is only slowly that the low and fearfully wretched condition of these people becomes fully known to one. Crime and cruelty seem so essentially inwrought and mingled with their very inmost lives that one feels obliged utterly and for ever to despair of all human ability to make them better. If good is done among them we will surely scorn to take the praise, for in our hearts we must say, 'It is the hand of the Lord, and only that— from beginning to end it is of the Lord.'

"A man came to me this morning to get some medicine, for both his ears were cut entirely off. He was charged with a crime which was indeed worthy of so severe a punishment, if he was guilty, but it ought to have been administered in a different way; but for it his master had this punishment inflicted. They cut and carve each other with a brutality which makes the heart sick. You see it everywhere. Scarcely a person passes you that cannot show the scars of some horrid wound. On each of the backs of two of our Christian women, as they walked from church before me last Sabbath, I remember to have seen, perhaps, three long, fearful scars. I am astonished, now, at the little I knew of the depths into which humanity can sink and indeed has sunk in all heathen lands. I speak not of occasional outbreaks into sin and crime, but of the deep, dark and settled wickedness of the human heart, and of the thorough and awful corruption which reaches to the very core and manifests itself everywhere. This, however, is the very thing which, instead of discouraging missionaries and Christians generally, ought to drive away all discouragement and doubt as to what we ought to do, and nerve every heart for earnest work, because it makes the path of duty so plain. It seems to say to every Christian, 'See here what guilt, what corruption, what wretchedness, what terrible misery, absolutely immeasurable woe!' Letting it alone will not help it; for centuries that course has been tried, and every hour it is let alone the guilt is becoming blacker, the corruption deeper, the wretchedness more wretched, the misery more awful; the degradation goes on and will go on, if you let it alone, until as a putrid mass the heathen world sinks in ruin. They cannot be helped, then, except we help them; give them the strength of the right hand; pull them out as from the fire by prayer and every means which God has ordained and will bless.

" But I did not intend to take up my paper with a sermon. I wish, however, I could preach in American ears some of the things I have felt since I came to Africa. I would like to take a section of Africa, with all its darkness and crime and sorrow and pitiable woe, and put it down in the midst of the people, that they might see. I think there would be some tears, some pity; I think there would be some warm and earnest resolves *to do*, some bitter regrets that more had not already been done.

" *December* 3.—This evening I returned from the Gaboon, where I had a short but pleasant visit. The missionaries there are kind-hearted, and make one feel as much at home as if they had been old friends. They have beautiful homes, and every comfort that could reasonably be desired. Their houses are built on high ground, back from and overlooking the river. They have a beautiful view of the sea, also, and of the ships as they lie at anchor in the river below.* The Gaboon is in possession of the French; they have built

---

* On the left of the engraving is the mission chapel, a pleasant bamboo structure, in the rear of which is the cemetery ; to the right of the hill stand the school-house and the mission residence.

GABOON STATION.

p. 218

quite a town on it, and have a considerable number of soldiers and government officers there. Several men-of-war also are kept constantly at the station. There are many English traders there also, which, with their ships lying in the river, give it the appearance of quite a business place. India rubber and ivory and palm oil are the chief articles of trade, and these are dealt in pretty largely. The Gaboon is an immense river, fifteen to twenty miles wide at the mouth. Even up where the town is and the mission station, it seems to be three or four miles wide. I did not find Mr. Mackey here, but we had letters from him saying that he was at Fernando Po, waiting for an opportunity to get down. His letters tell us that he is not much better. The physician at Sierra Leone told him that he could not live in Africa, and that if he wished to save his life he had better return to America as soon as possible.

"I found my letters at the Gaboon; and surely I have not had such a gloomy package in many respects since I came to Africa. The death of Aunt S. was very, very saddening, and so entirely unexpected. I do not yet realize it; it seems such a terrible breaking of old associations and plans of happiness which you all had doubtless formed in having her so near. So she is gone ! I look back with strange feelings to see how our friends are crumbling away—one and another dropping into the grave, and leaving great blanks in our hearts which nothing on earth can fill."

After referring to the death of several other friends, he says : "The wheel of Providence keeps turning majestically on, breaking up for ever the surface of social life, and crushing beneath it unsparingly each one's most cherished plans ; and this is only kindness to us on God's part—he chastens only because he loves ; if he designed to ruin us, he would simply leave us alone.

"But I almost forgot these sorrows in the joy that I found when I read that James had united with the church. I had been long waiting and asking for it. I trust it will not be long until Joseph gives his heart to God. Every day that a Christian lives he sees more and more the wisdom of his choice, and only wonders that he forgot his God so long. He that has acted the most wisely in life is the one who has given his heart the soonest to God—given it wholly.

"*December* 13.—I am sitting in my study to-day, writing up for the mail; for I expect to go and visit the out-stations again next week. I hear the wild pigeons cooing all around and the birds trilling most beautiful songs. The wild flowers cover the ground just before the door, and the air is as pleasant as on any June day at home. It is a great mistake to suppose that Africa is such a desolate, dreary land as some imagine—scorched with hot suns and stifling winds, and covered with burning sands. I would almost venture to say, that in most respects there is not a more delightful land on the face of the globe. If your early June days, with their green fields and fresh air and singing birds, lasted all the year round, then you would realize something of the beauty and pleasantness of Africa. I do not know that I have seen the thermometer above 80°, and when the sun would be hottest we usually have clouds to temper its beams; and then the fresh sea breeze always gives life to the atmosphere about us. But if I said no more than this I would not tell you the whole truth; for you would think that in such a land as I have described one might be for ever renewing his youth, and have good hopes of living to a great age. But not so; while Africa carries beauty in her right hand, she holds death in her left—she poisons while she pleases. It seems strange that, in a land so lovely, white men wither away until they become thin, sallow, care-worn shadows ; and yet they hardly know why, and, indeed, are scarcely conscious of the change that is going on, so subtle and deadly is the poison. I suppose it arises from the constant decay of vegetable matter, from which poisonous gases rise up and mingle in every breath we draw.

"We have a Scotch botanist and conchologist staying with us for a few days, making some collections. He has been pointing out some plants new to me, as the arrow-root, which grows abundantly all around, and the castor-oil plant, from the bean of which castor-oil is made.

"*December* 15.—To-day, for recreation, Dr. Nassau proposed a little boat ride to a beautiful island half a mile in extent and a mile or two out at sea. We took the school children and the ladies along. Just as we were nearly there we saw a vessel about to anchor near Corisco. So as soon as we were landed at the little island, I took the boat and boatmen and went to bring Mr. Mackey ashore, for we knew that he was aboard the vessel. Everybody was glad to see him back again, for he is greatly beloved here. His health is not much better, and it is not likely that he will be able to stay here long."

From Mr. Paull's diary we take the following brief notes:

"*December* 20.—To-day just recovering from the eighth attack of fever. Am preparing to go again on my trip to Benita. Am reading Wordsworth's 'Excursion.'

"*December* 22.—Started again with Dr. Nassau for Benita. Arrived at Aje. Had a full house to preach to. Bought a little house.

"*December* 23.—Reached Benita in the evening. Preached to a great houseful.

"*December* 24.—Spent the day in examining the grounds in search of a site for the mission-house. Came on fresh elephant and deer tracks.

"*December* 25.—Christmas. Preached twice at Benita and visited towns up the coast, talking to the people.

"*December* 26.—Left Benita and reached Hanje. Had a long walk along the beach, and dined on roasted corn.

"*December* 27.—Reached Aje again. Started in the night for Eloby.

"*December* 28.—Reached Eloby in the night. Sick at Eloby.

"*December* 29. — Reached Corisco about 10 o'clock.

"*December* 31.—Preached in church at Evangasimba on Christian earnestness. Preparatory sermon to communion.

"*January* 1, 1865.—Communion. Large turnout of people. One baptism—Ndate's wife.

"*January* 8.—Busy making preparations to go and live on the mainland at the mouth of the Benita River, where the mission a few days ago appointed me to go and build a station that I might the better overlook the mainland stations."

To his mother he writes from Corisco, January 12, 1865:

"I think I was just about preparing for another trip to Benita when I finished my last letter to you. Dr. Nassau went with me, and we had in many respects a most delightful trip, though the doctor was sick most of the time; he cannot bear the tossings of the sea. Nausea does not now trouble me, and I can eat on the boat when out for a whole day. I think I shall become quite a boatman after a while, as my work among the stations will call me almost constantly up and down the coast.

"Our trip this time was partly to examine the point at the mouth of the Benita River on which we propose to build a permanent station. We spent two days there, one of which was the Sabbath. On Saturday we looked for a site to build, and selected a beautiful point right in the angle between the mouth of the river and the sea. I think I have scarcely seen a more attractive spot on the coast of Africa. The cool and refreshing sea-breeze sweeps over it constantly, and behind there is a broad and beautiful plain entirely free from trees with the exception of a cluster here and there. A grassy plain is one of the rarest and most attractive sights in Africa, and we think that such a spot near to one's home adds more to one's health than anything else, on account of the absence of decaying vegetation. The site is tolerably elevated, and gives you a view of the sea that stretches far away to the west. There is not much doubt that this will be altogether as healthy a place as on the island. The traders who live across the river enjoy excellent health. The people are quiet and most kindly disposed, and withal most anxious to have a missionary.

" I brought down four boys to school this trip, and was to bring my friend Tom's little wife, of whom I wrote in my last letter, but when we were about to start and Tom looked for his wife she was nowhere to be found. She had run off to hide herself. At last, when we were just getting in the boat, Tom saw her away up the beach and ran to fetch her, but she was off like an antelope, and so I had to come without her. Tom seemed mortified at the mishap, as he had already asked for a passage by my *next* trip to come down and see his wife at Corisco. The wind was very much against us, and we made only a few miles in the day. When we sailed five or six miles we sailed to shore and walked along the beach to Hanje, and let the men row the boat. This walk was a pleasant little episode in our trip. We landed at a little new town, ground for which had just been cleared out of the heavy timber. The people all (twenty or thirty in number) came down to the shore, and by their bright, happy faces seemed to give us a hearty welcome. As the tide was full along the beach we concluded to wait an hour or so till it should go down. As we had brought a bucket of provisions from the boat, we sat down and ate. Around the town was about an acre of corn just ready to roast. So we had three ears apiece roasted and sat down on native stools in front of the headman's house to enjoy our feast, the people all about us in a circle, delighted and making merry. Before we commenced to eat we each asked a silent blessing, and there was a hush among some of the people and a quiet murmur, as though they were inquiring among themselves what it meant. One of the women who had somewhere learned something of religion, immediately said 'Akalakia' (he prays).

"We had salt for our corn, but no butter. The fat from a cooked ham, however, melted on the hot corn, answered in its place. One of the women sympathized with the doctor in his seasickness, and went through the motion of seasickness to show him how boat-riding always affected her. When we had finished our meal and sat a little while, we had prayer with them, and spoke to them of the gospel, and then went on our way, leaving them delighted, and delighted ourselves with the visit. I do not remember to have had a more pleasant little interlude in Africa. The doctor was weak and could only walk slowly, and was obliged to rest often, so we were after night getting to Hanje. The latter part of the way was rough and rocky, and we had a creek to cross into which I tumbled in the darkness and was wet above the knees. I suffered no inconvenience from it, however, for we soon got to the mission station, and I took off my wet clothes and put on a pair of Njumba's pants and went to bed. The boat did not arrive till late at night.

"We had to cross also a river about a hundred yards wide; but over this we were ferried in a canoe. There was a large town on the opposite bank and plenty of people gathered about us; to these also we preached the gospel. Some of them followed us a short distance and then gave us their parting salutation, which is, 'keke bwamu' (go, good), something like our 'fare ye well.' I like the people for their simplicity and kindness of heart. Sometimes an incident occurs among them to make one laugh. As we were sitting beside rather a fierce-looking old headman on the Benita, suddenly he took us by the beards, and, shaking them vigorously, said we ought to cut them off, especially about the mouth, as he thought it must hinder one greatly in eating. Most white men here allow the whole beard to grow, thinking it perhaps more healthy, and indeed not caring to shave. But few of the natives have any beard, except perhaps a little tuft on the chin; and they greatly envy the long beards of the white men, and some of them say, 'God is not good to them because he gave them so little.' Some of the boys inquire very earnestly if there is not something in the white man's country that can be rubbed on the face to make the beard grow.

"We started from Hanje about 4 o'clock in the morning so as to get the land breeze, but did not even then reach Aje till late in the evening. After two or three hours' rest at Aje, we set off again about 11 or 12 o'clock in the night, so as to have the land breeze and tide in our favor. By hard sailing we reached Eloby at 8 o'clock in the night, and from there we were glad to get back to Corisco by the next morning, having been gone over a week.

"I greatly love the missonary work in Africa. I do not know that I have ever been so completely happy in any work as in this. My prayer is that God may spare me here for many years. The people are deeply in need of the word of life, perishing sadly without it; and, alas! we are so few and our hands so feeble that we cannot do a tithe of the work that it seems criminal to leave undone. Mr. Mackey is back, and his health is much better. This gives me a joyful release from so much secular labor, and now I am about to enter fully on the work that in my heart I love. In your last letter you asked me not to go to the mainland. I think I can appreciate your feelings and sympathize with you in them. But you can scarcely realize the necessity that we feel here for pushing on the work among the tribes that yet sit in darkness. Our hearts burn to raise the torch higher and carry it farther, until it shall gladden the tribes who now perish in gloom. We came here to serve God and to do his work ; so death cannot touch us, nor even the floods drown us, until God is ready ; and when God is ready, then 'it is well.' You will not be grieved, then, I know, when I tell you that God has brought me into high honor, the highest by far of my life—that is, to leave my home and comforts again, and go to live among the heathen anew. This will not give you sorrow, I know, because it will give me more happiness and joy than aught else almost that I could name on earth. The mission, at our last meeting, appointed me as the pioneer of the work on the mainland. Others would willingly have gone, but God gave the privilege to me, and indeed his providence has gradually been opening up my way ever since I came.

"For the last few days I have been packing boxes with tools for building and goods for trade, and next week I am to set sail for the mouth of the Benita, that beautiful spot on which I am to build. Mr. and Mrs. Mackey will possibly take the trip with me, and see me safely landed. I shall take

BUILDING AT BENITA.

p. 231.

everything along that will be needful for my present comfort, and perhaps I may also get back to civilization every two or three months. Mrs. Mackey and Mrs. M'Queen will supply me with cooking apparatus, and I will get plenty of provisions from the storehouse: so you need have no uneasiness about these things. As for loneliness, that will not trouble me, and the slight fevers which sometimes come I have learned to check; so with trust in God I shall do well.

"The plan of my house I have drawn off to send you. It is to be built of bamboo, with board floors. The reception-room is made large, as it will be the preaching place. The kitchen will be outside, and a little hut will answer for that. It is to be built above ground on mangrove posts. I suppose it will take about two months to finish it, and in the mean time I expect to live in a native house. So far as comforts go I shall have enough in every way, for I will not expect many. But I shall be able to tell you more fully of my situation in my next letter.

"Our new mission station among the Kombes will require some outlay, and the Board is pressed for funds. If matters become worse, I think I could live on half my salary, and I would gladly do it to help on the cause; but this need not have been spoken of. For the present press, however, we greatly need a new boat; it will cost perhaps two hundred and fifty dollars, and we propose if possible to raise it by private contribution. Cousin L. B. by the last mail wrote to me to let her know if I needed anything, so I am sure she will contribute, and Dr. Nassau will perhaps write to some friends. If any of our friends, or the friends of missions in the church at home, cared to do anything, it would be a gratification and a great help to the cause. I am sure God will not let us sink, but will put it into the hearts of some who love his name to help on the work.

"P. S.—*January* 17.—I must append a note on the eve of starting. In the morning I expect to go. We had a delightful prayer-meeting to-night which strengthened my heart, and I go to my work full of peace and joy, and hopeful that I may gather some sheaves from the great ripened harvest. Do not think of me as in the least sad or lonely. I almost feel sure that I shall not be either. God has been preparing me hitherto for all that is to come upon me. I shall have good company in the presence of Him who has said, 'I will never leave thee nor forsake thee.' 'Lo, I am

with you alway, even unto the end of the world.'
And I doubt not I will learn more of this kind
friend when my fellowship must be almost solely
with him. I seem almost to be going out as a missionary anew; I have all the joy of such a step, and
it gives me a little sadness, too, at parting with my
brethren and sisters. Much love, etc.

"Geo. Paull."

He wrote under date of February 15 to Mr. and
Mrs. Mackey concerning the new mission station at
Benita. "The place grows in beauty. I think I
am safe in saying that I have seen no place on the
face of the earth that so gladdened my heart. Its
beauty, along with the general good progress of
everything, has kept me entirely from growing
lonely or even sick, except the slightest possible
attack of fever. I trust that the outward prosperity which thus far seems to attend and encourage the work here may be a forecasting of the spiritual blessings that may follow when the station
is fully manned and the work thoroughly entered
into.

"The attendance at church continues most encouraging. Quite a number were down from
Meduma last Sabbath. Though there was rain

in the morning, yet about one hundred and twenty found their way out to church."

The following note to Mrs. Clemens, at Corisco, is from Benita River Station, February 16, 1871:

"I did not have time by the last boat to drop you a reply to your kind note of the second. I was glad to get it. Kind words and assurances of friendly regard are of wondrous worth, and my package of letters will never be so large but that I will be glad to have others added by friends at Corisco.

"There is much that is cheering about the work among this people, and it is really delightful to be among them. I know this is ploughing in new soil, and one cannot judge from first appearances what the more permanent state of things may be. But for the present, at least, everything is exceedingly encouraging; and indeed I do not know why they should not always remain so; I mean if we do our part. I have exceeding faith in the faithfulness of God. If he has said he will give his spirit I think he means it; I think too he is far more willing to save souls than we are to have them saved. When, therefore, there is deadness in the church and sinners are not being converted, the fault is not God's but ours. I do believe in my heart that if we missionaries and all Christians lived as I am sure we ought to live, and as some have lived, there would be a revival all the year round, and sinners would be inquiring the way to Zion all the while. God's faithfulness and his promises in the Scriptures fully warrant such a belief. When no blessings come down we are apt to throw the blame on God, but do it in the form of a modest apology for him, saying, 'His time is not come yet.' I am ashamed whenever I think this, for it is dishonoring to God. It is casting on him that which only results from our own indolence and lack of spirituality. God's time to glorify himself and save sinners is always here. I believe there is no time when he is more ready than at any other."

Extracts from his journal:

"*January* 18.—God has given me to see this, one of the gladdest days of my life. This morning I sailed from Corisco to build my home among the heathen at the mouth of the Benita on the mainland. Mr. and Mrs. Mackey came with me as far as Hanje, where we arrived at dark. We brought two boats, which carried my building tools, clothing, food and goods for purchases. Mrs. Mackey and Mrs. M'Queen have shown great kindness in fitting me out with everything necessary for housekeeping. I take Upingalo along for cook and housekeeper.

"*January* 19.—This morning, after breakfast at Hanje, the people came together to talk their palaver with us for passing by them and going to Benita River. We explained our reasons fully, but they were not satisfied, and declared if we did not build with them that the Scripture readers must leave, and that the house and everything must be taken away. They had made threats against the Scripture readers, and had declared that they would burn or tear down their house. We told them that our plans were already made and that talking was useless; so about 10 o'clock I started with the boats and men, leaving Mr. and Mrs. Mackey there to await the return of the larger one. Reached Benita about 10 o'clock and met with a most joyous welcome. Every one seemed overflowing with gladness. They gave me gladly the best house in town to live in, and ran with great haste to carry up my boxes and stow them away. Upingalo arranged things nicely, and at tea-time set me a nice table with snow-white cloth and tea-set. He brought me coffee with goat's milk, butter and good bread and ham, which Mrs.

Mackey had provided; tea-cakes, a large tin of which Mrs. M'Queen had made me, served as a kind of dessert. My house is tolerably neat and clean. It is bamboo, good size, with one outside door, but no windows save a little one about two feet by ten inches. I am provided with a good mattress, blankets and mosquito-net.

"I had a houseful at prayers — read and explained part of the first chapter of Genesis. May God make me a blessing to this people!

"*January* 20.—This morning I arose refreshed by a tolerably good sleep. After breakfast I took some men to cut a path and went to look at a place for building. I selected one of the most charming spots, I think, I have ever seen—a bluff about fifteen or twenty feet high and about one hundred yards back from the beach. On the top of the bluff the land is almost level, and runs back about a mile in a beautiful plateau of almost entirely clear land. The view from it extends into the river and away over the sea. A strong and constant sea-breeze sweeps over it almost day and night. To-morrow the king and headmen are to meet me and sell me the land, and I commence to build. The old king and several headmen were to see me this afternoon. They say they are very glad to have some one to live among them and teach them about God and how to be good, for some of the people are very bad.

"The man whose house Upingalo uses for a kitchen came to see how much I would pay him for the use of it. He thought he ought to have two dollars a month, but at last agreed to come at the end of a month and receive one dollar. I went with Ume (the carpenter) this afternoon and cut the fork of a tree to hang the grindstone on. The next thing will be to set and file the saw, so as to be ready for building.

"The house that I now live in is quite comfortable. The large room, which I use as a reception-room, study, dining-room and sitting-room, is about fourteen by sixteen feet. The walls are about eight feet high, and there is no ceiling between me and the rafters. The rain, as it pours down to-night, knocks the soot from the roof on the paper, but Upingalo will remedy that soon by the use of a broom. The other room is about eight feet by twelve, and has no window or door to admit the light except a little one three feet by one-half. This is nearly always closed to keep out the thieves, for here our treasures are kept. It is pantry and store-house and bed-room. Chests and dishes and trade-goods and bread and meat, etc., are all stowed here. The whole house has a floor of newly-pounded clay, which is comfortable enough and looks clean. I had a board tied up in the large room for books, etc., and another in the small one to put the dishes on. There is a rope stretched across the room on which to hang coats, towels, etc.

"As I came in from cutting the grindstone frame I found a pile of bark burning away like a small coal-pit, and when I inquired I found it was a miniature pottery. They make very nice vessels for water, holding about a quart, out of clay, figured over on the outside, and very much the shape of a small iron pot. When they have made them they put them into a pile and pile bark around to burn them. When done they are quite hard and serviceable. They make pipes in the same way—pipes, too, that show the skill of an artist.

" I saw some men and women this evening going out to watch all night in their gardens, which are about half a mile away. This is the only way they can keep the elephants from destroying their food. I tried to show them how they might dig pits at their crossing places and catch the elephants, but that seems to them too much trouble. All the old garden-spots that I see have the remains of a lodge where the night watchers slept." The reader will at once be reminded of that passage in Isa. i. 8, "The daughter of Zion is left as a cottage in a vineyard, as a lodge in a garden of cucumbers."

"We had a full house at prayers, and I read and spoke to attentive listeners about the creation of man. The three native Christians that came with me gathered into my room after prayers, and we sang Benga hymns together till 8 o'clock. They had no desire to leave off, although they had not yet had their suppers. It is a delightful thing to have these Christians with me—they seem like brethren indeed in a land of heathen. I hope they will do great good among the people. To-day I set Mbata (the Scripture reader) to teaching a school, which he has been doing in some sort before. Big men and little boys go and are busy learning the A, B, C. Some of them, too, have now learned to spell. A headman from across the river came to see me to-day and brought me a present of a chicken, and I had, of course, to give him in return a present worth more than the chicken.

"I have an almanac for 1865 which Mr. Mackey

brought out and presented me. This keeps my time as to the days and weeks, and I have a big silver watch which I bought from Mr. Mackey. This tells me how the hours go. For calling the people together for prayers, I have a shrill whistle (for we have no bell as yet) which Mr. M'Queen used and which Mrs. M'Queen gave me. I hope to hand this back to her, however, whenever anybody is kind enough to send us a bell from America.

"The missionaries in Corisco feel a great interest in this mainland undertaking, and they treated me with great kindness and did everything for my comfort that they could when I left. Surely it is not vain and dishonest talk when I say that I cannot see why God should treat me so kindly and give me every comfort and enjoyment that I need, so that in this land of darkness I am as truly happy, I think, as I have ever been in my brightest days at home, among friends that I love and surrounded by whatever we thought could make life enjoyable.

"*January* 21.—This morning the old king and the headmen came together to sell me some ground for the mission buildings. I sat down and told them my object in coming among them, and what

16

I would expect on their part, viz., a good attendance on missionary instructions, and when their people stole anything from me that they were to have it returned, also that I was to have a voice in their palavers and councils, etc., etc., to all of which they agreed. Poor people! I feel greatly attached to them; and they are very kind, and yielded almost everything to me that I asked. They are wonderfully anxious to have a missionary among them, and say they want very much to be taught about God. Mine will be a fearfully responsible work. I shall need grace every hour.

"The land thus bought for the mission, I think, is the most beautiful spot on which my eye ever fell. Among the hills of Pennsylvania or the prairies of the West or amid the rich scenery of Scotland I do not think I ever saw anything that made my heart so glad. Beautiful, beautiful, beautiful, is all I can say that would be anything like an adequate description. I went out this afternoon and stretched myself on its green sward under the shade of a tree, and as I looked up I am sure my heart swelled with gladness that I was in a land so lovely and engaged in a work so blessed. I scarcely get time to sit down for a moment but the people gather about me, and if I commence to learn the language from them their faces grow bright and they take great delight in helping me.

"On the land are two springs which the people say never go dry. I was careful to have them within the line, so that there might be no failure of water. Near one of them I notice there are four different varieties of beautiful wild flowers, which, if they could be transplanted to America, would be esteemed treasures.

"*January* 22.—This has been a delightful Sabbath. I spent the morning in thinking over the first three chapters of Genesis. At 10 o'clock and at night in my sermons I dwelt on the creation and fall and the evil of the heart as described by Paul in the first chapter of Romans, trying at the same time to give some impression of the greatness and sovereignty of God. I think these most important subjects just at the beginning of my work. Both morning and night I had fixed attention; at night, especially, it seemed very solemn. At morning service there was an audience of between seventy and eighty people, crowded together in the little native house and about the door. One, at least, and perhaps more, came a distance of eight or ten miles to hear the gospel. I asked him if his heart believed the things he had heard. He said, 'Yes, or else I would not come so far to hear.' At night there were about fifty present. I started a Sabbath-school in the afternoon, to which about thirty men, women and children came. The native Christians taught them a while, and then I spent the rest of the time in trying to explain to them the way of salvation. My friend Tom seems seriously attentive, and the young men tell me this evening that he has been asking them to teach him how to pray. Perhaps God will bless our work here, and then the prayers that I have tried to offer for a long time will be answered. I will pray and work and wait. I trust God will yet use me for his glory. The people in town have behaved in a very orderly way, and with great apparent respect for the day of God.

"*January* 23.—This Monday active work commences in the way of preparation for the new house, and it makes quite a stir about the little town, for every one is anxious to earn a cloth or a hat, etc. Out of the number of applicants I hired some twenty. Part of them went to cut and carry posts to set the house on, the remainder with their cutlasses I set to clearing off the ground, cutting away bushes and making a road to the beach. Some of the number are women, and they hack away with their cutlasses as well as the men, when the work is light. They form a merry group of workmen. I have been among them most of the day showing them what to do. In the evening they gathered about my house to know how much they were to be paid.

"Upingalo (the cook) thinks he has too much to do; so Ngombalonda came to-night (a nice bright boy, who had been Mrs. M'Queen's table and pantry boy), and he is to stay and help and go on with his studies. I let him stay, chiefly in hope that I might be able to do him some good. I am to teach the four mission boys, Upingalo, Ume, Mbata and Ngombalonda, in the evenings. As they are all Christians except the last, I find great pleasure in having them about me. I read a chapter with them in Benga, and explain it as we go along. Beside this, they are to study geography and arithmetic, etc. This is in my own room. We have public prayers every morning and evening, which many people attend. I read a chapter and discourse on it, and we then sing a hymn and have prayer.

"While the young men were in my room

to-night, they asked me if I had a father. I said 'Yes,' and showed them his picture. They looked at it and said, 'Ah, he is a good man, very good. He is old; he was a good man when he was young.'

" *Upingalo*—'Tell him Upingalo says he is an old man.'

" *Ume*—'Tell him when I go to America I will see him. This face looks like yours.'

" Age is the great thing in a man, with them, which demands reverence and respect. I had a letter from Mr. Mackey to-day, saying that the trouble at Hanje was all amicably settled before he left.

" *January* 24.—This evening closes a busy day, and also brings a good deal of weariness with it. I have about twenty-five workmen on my list who require to have everything that is to be done marked out for them; and then they are to be watched while they are at it, lest they make a mistake. I have four out of the twenty-five posts on which the house is to stand already in the ground, and to-morrow evening I hope to have the rest. We put them down three feet in the ground. I try to find out the best and most sensible workmen, and then act as headman for the rest. Plenty of

spectators come and stand about to see what is going on. The patent tape-line and the spirit-level
call forth wonderful admiration. I am having a
road cut around the ground; in some places the
workmen actually have to tunnel through the thick
bush, leaving a perfect roof of bushes and limbs
overhead.

"Our evening prayer was delightful to-night;
over thirty were present, to whom I spoke about
half an hour plainly and personally. I never saw
more fixed attention and more unmistakable interest in what was said. I cannot but hope that
God will bless his truth to the people. One man
spoke in reply for the rest, and his words showed
that the truths they had heard were setting them
to thinking.

"*January* 25.—The list of workmen has in-
creased to thirty to-day. They work faithfully,
carrying tremendous loads of timber, as much
as twelve of them can stagger along with. They
are good-natured and even jolly. The women hack
away with their cutlasses, though they do not accomplish very much. I sent four of them this
morning to cut a path on the other side of a ravine
near where we are building the house. But from
some superstitious notion they were afraid to go.

They said men might work there, but they would die if they went. We came to a place the other day from which the men, king, headman and all ran away. They said they had buried a tiger there, and if anybody went to that spot it would bring sickness on the people. So they made a law that whoever went there should pay a great fine.

"One of the headmen brought me a present of a chicken yesterday, and old King Mango, who lives two or three miles up the coast, came to see me to-day where we are building. He brought me a present of a chicken and a large bunch of plantains. I seated his majesty on a block and gave him my umbrella to keep the sun off. When I got leisure I came with him to the house where I live (one-quarter of a mile away), and made him a present of a fine butcher-knife, with which he was greatly delighted. I hope to win the hearts of the people by kindness, and then I shall have the better opportunity for doing them good.

"*January* 26.—This morning the rain hindered us, but we got something done notwithstanding. All the posts are in the ground, and we have commenced putting on the sills. This is wearing work, as it is difficult to hew and make them fit properly. I came to dinner perfectly exhausted,

but after a hearty meal and a short rest I felt as
fresh as ever.   One of the headmen brought me a
present of a chicken and a bunch of plantains.   I
suppose he was tempted by my present to the king
yesterday.   I gave him a hat.   Getting presents
of chickens and plantains is very expensive, as I
have to give a *dash* of double their worth in return.
I have the men now cutting a path direct from
where we are working to the town.   I suppose the
people will be glad of that.   They never go to the
trouble of cutting a path if they can avoid it.
They prefer to go half a mile round.

" *January* 27.—This morning another headman
brought me a present, a basket of corn and a leg
of venison.   The venison was something of a
rarity, though the bush abounds with a beautiful
little deer which the people sometimes shoot.   A
pair of pheasants flew up before me to-day, but I
scarcely got to see them enough to say what they
were like.   I saw yesterday a most beautiful
bird, black, with red bill and a white ring round
its neck.   It had five or six long tail-feathers,
perhaps six inches long.   Its body was no larger
than a snow-bird.

" The work at the mission-house is progressing.
The three heavy sills running the whole length of

the house are hewn and nailed on. Much of the
fitting of timbers and hewing I am obliged to do
myself; and in the evenings I feel almost exhausted.
The men keep in good spirits, and upon the whole
are the best Africans to work that I have ever seen.
Old King Mango and some of the headmen came to
see me this evening to put their marks to the deed
and get their pay for the ground. I promised to be
ready for them to-morrow.

"The morning and evening prayers are well
attended. This evening over thirty were present.
I try to teach them and explain the Scriptures as I
go along.

"A man came to me to-day to see if I could doctor his wife's arm. By some means the shaft of an
arrow had been driven through it. I told him to
bring her and I would try and do something to
help it.

"*January* 28.—To-day came another present
from a headman, of a bunch of plantains and a
chicken. In the afternoon also another headman
brought me a part of a large fish. I set the workmen free about the middle of the afternoon, as
they had been working hard and faithfully all the
week; and as I myself was tired, and had beside
appointed this afternoon to meet the headmen to

pay them for the land, and write them a 'big book' (a kind of deed), a copy of which I keep for myself also. I had written, on the day we went around the land, a small article, just to seal the bargain. I paid the six headmen and the king four pieces of cloth, two shirts, six knives and a few other things, all of which in America would cost about ten dollars. These they divided among themselves. I made as presents also (tokens of friendship) six large butcher knives to the headmen, and to the king I gave a red shirt. As we went around the path again we came across the bones of a great elephant which had been killed a long time ago.

"*January* 29.—This has been a delightful Sabbath. In the morning I preached to a congregation of considerably over a hundred people crowded into the house and about the door. Preached on the Lord's Prayer. Two of the traders were over from the other side of the river, the only English traders there, and about twenty people beside. They were most attentive, and I cannot but hope that God will bless his truth plainly spoken. The traders stayed with me for dinner. In the afternoon we had a prayer meeting, and at night preaching again to a good and attentive audience. Our singing has been delightful. One of the Scripture readers with his wife from Hanje was here, and one also from Aje. Ngombalonda, one of the mission boys, is my clerk. He knows many tunes and sings very well. My own singing powers are developing somewhat.

"*January* 30.—To-day I have been sick and scarcely able to attend to building. The hot sun this morning I think brought it on. A leopard came into town last night and killed a goat. The people are a good deal afraid of the leopards.

"*February* 1.—Yesterday I was sick with a slight attack of fever, but heavy doses of quinine have made me feel quite well to-day. The work of building goes on prosperously. Last night was a sleepless night on account of the fever, which was just leaving me. Ume says, ' Ah, Mr. Paull, the people of America make us very sorry, they catch our grandfather and carry him away, they carry away our people' (alluding to the slave traders).

"*February* 3.—This is my twenty-ninth birthday (I am twenty-eight years old), and I have spent it as much as possible in quietness and alone, telling the men to get along as best they could without me. It was almost impossible to have ten minutes of quiet in town, so I went out into the bush. The natives gathered about me to-night in the bright moonlight, while I told them some things about the sun, moon and stars. They asked why they could see no stars when the moon was round. They thought it was because all the stars then gathered themselves together to the moon to increase its brightness.

"*February* 5.—The Mange came this morning with the mail. She had been delayed by a tornado. The people did not create an excitement as they would have done on another day. It rained this morning, and I expected scarcely any out to church, but God sent me one hundred and ten. I think I never preached so stumblingly since I came to Africa. But God can bless the poorest effort.

"The Christians tell me to-night that two of the natives have been asking them how to pray with all their hearts. They say their hearts never troubled them as they do now. May God now commence the work among us!

"*Sabbath*, February 12.—This has been a good day. The attendance at church was one hundred and twenty—many more than I hoped for, as it rained in the morning. Preached on Isaiah, fifty-fifth chapter. In the afternoon meeting for prayer, and at night, there was an attendance of from thirty to fifty, and most solemn attention as I preached on the personal responsibility of those who hear the word of God.

"*February* 18.—This evening Isanga came—one of the men whose ' heart has been troubling him.' He says, ' I heard from Mbata about heaven and hell and sin and death, but I did not understand about Christ. When you came and told us about Christ suffering and dying to save us sinners, and about his being the Son of God and coming to die in our places, I asked my heart if it was its sin that made Christ die, and ever since my heart troubled me.' Mbala came in and I spoke with him; he says that he believes the truths that he hears, but they do not trouble him. However, he seems to be trying to pray. Upingalo says he heard him praying the other night at midnight. He says the young men are also beginning to pray. Tom prays at midnight, and prays a good deal. O Spirit, breathe on the bones in this valley! Jesus seems to help one wonderfully when he walks in the path of duty. I have never in my life seemed to be enabled to make the way of salvation so plain as since I came among the people of Africa. Every day almost my heart is whispering, 'Hasten, hasten, hasten; do not lose a day! You know that life in Africa is short, and there is much to be done. Do not let your time be taken up with any trifles, but hasten on the main work—preach the gospel.'

"*February* 19.—This seemed a barren day to my soul. No desires after God, heart hard and immovable, with no strength to do anything good, but always failing in my good resolves to do for God. So I felt until dark, when God was pleased to visit me and soften my feelings, and although I felt so worthless, as having done not a thing that could stand before God in all my life, yet I thought in the last day it might appear that he had used my efforts some little for his glory—that possibly he might have enabled me to be of a little comfort to some of his people. But I felt so weary of sin and temptation and failure to glorify God as I ought that I earnestly prayed to Jesus, if it be his will, to take me to himself out of the world. I thought of myself as having sinned against God from my birth, and yet God pitied me and bore with me and would not cut me off, but sent his Son to die for me. When I thought of the wonderful forbearance of God my heart was melted to tears.

"To-night I preached on 'God so loved the world,' etc. Preached with some degree of feeling and warmth, and the people were most attentive. After service I asked those who wished to talk about Christ to stay, or those who wished to inquire how they might be saved. Some twenty remained. I asked if they all remained to talk about Christ, and they said that they did. Six of them said their hearts had been troubling them on account of their sins. One man said he would not speak about himself now, but he would pray on and pray on and pray on until Christ changed his heart, and then he would come and tell me of it. Several women remained who seemed seriously disposed; one expressed a desire to be a Christian. Preached this morning on the fifty-first Psalm— about seventy-five people present. Talked in the afternoon prayer-meeting about heaven and its desirableness.

"*Monday*, February 20.—Oh, I am struck dumb with strange feelings! I believe God is working by his Spirit among this people. To-night after prayers, at which there was a large attendance, the houseful seemed to stand still and sit down again as though not ready to leave. I, however, came on into my own little home, and three or four of those who expressed concern last night followed me and sat down, seeming desirous to speak, so I spoke with them and found them apparently much concerned. Others came in to the number of nine—every one declaring himself to be concerned and troubled on account of his sins—Ebuma, Miodi, Madoha, Beduka, Ikuba, Ijabi, Upinda, Jumna, Ngambalonda. I spent, perhaps, an hour and a half talking with each one and trying to show them the way to Christ. O God, my heart is full! I would hide myself away in the dust! Do thou work for thyself among this people! Some of them say that their trouble arises from a feeling that they have a sinful heart. Ebuma says he has always wondered where he was to go to when he died, and now he hears of heaven and hell and is troubled, and wishes to find the way to heaven.

" *Tuesday*, 21st.—O Lord my God, I do not know what to say. I ought to hide my face in the dust, and I feel like hiding away from thy presence, lest by some word or act or neglect of duty I should grieve thy spirit, if indeed thou hast commenced to work among this people. But, O Lord, if it is thy work, thou hast commenced it and thou wilt not suffer my follies to stop it. Thou wilt

17

not suffer anything to stop it, but wilt carry it on to thy name's everlasting glory. Glory, glory be unto thee, O God! Thou livest and reignest in mercy and kindness; this is my hope.

"This evening there was a much larger attendance than usual on prayers, and the people were solemnly attentive. They had no disposition to rise and go away after it was over. I spoke to them of their danger and lost condition, and tried to show them that Christ was their only helper, and urged them to seek him. Five followed me into my room to inquire the way to Christ—Beduka and his wife, Bela (1) and Bela (2) and Tom. They seem to be really concerned for their souls' salvation. Some of them have a most clear view of their lost and helpless and sinful condition. I am astonished at their Scriptural knowledge of their state. O God, revive thy work! Saviour, pour down thy spirit as showers upon the mown grass!

"*February* 22.—To-night was our prayer-meeting. The attendance was as large as it usually is on Sabbath evenings at church. I spoke on Acts, chapter second, 'Out-pouring of the spirit, and call to repentance.' Some remained to make inquiries how they might be saved. The words of Isanga and Ebuma were especially interesting and encouraging.

"*February* 23.—Oh God, I am filled with wonder at thy ways of dealing! Who by searching can find out God? Art thou in very deed visiting this people with the reviving influence of thy spirit? A full house at prayers, to which I spoke at considerable length on the 'Barren fig-tree and the strait gate.' Surely I never saw more fixed and solemn attention, but no display of feeling. I was enabled to speak very solemnly and pointedly. I invited those who wished to ask any questions or to talk about Christ to come into my room. Five followed me. Two of them, Bomani and Besaka, had never spoken with me before, the other three had. All the young men in town seem to be praying. They are heard at midnight lifting up their voices to God in prayer. Almost every one who has come to me has made this remark: 'We heard from the Scripture reader before about God and heaven and hell, and our hearts did not trouble us, but since you told us about Christ we feel trouble in our hearts.' One noble young fellow, whom I have noticed apparently much interested, came last night and said with much earnestness, 'Tell me how to pray.' To-night he came again with every indication of deepest earnestness and said, 'I come to ask you how to love Christ. My heart keeps saying, Love Christ! love Christ! Tell me how to love him.' The deep sincerity of this young man is most interesting. 'I came to tell you before that my heart was in trouble, but now it troubles me more and more. It did not trouble me until I heard the things you told us about Christ.' One young man came who has been much concerned for two or three weeks and was one of the first two. There are some things that seem hopeful in his case; perhaps he has been led to believe. The most surprising thing about these young men is their Scriptural knowledge, although until November last they had never heard the gospel, with the exception of a few who had heard something of it from a Scripture reader at Meduma. God's spirit, I am convinced, must himself have taught them the things they know.

"*Sabbath*, February 26.—To-day I have tried to preach the gospel to perishing sinners. There was in the morning a congregation of more than a hundred. I preached on 'The Son of man is come to seek and to save,' etc. Many listened with fixed and earnest attention. In the afternoon prayer-meeting I spoke on 'The kindness and love of Christ,' as shown in healing those who came to him. There was much earnest attention by all, and some apparent tenderness. Oh that the word of Christ might enter into their hearts, and that the power of the Holy Ghost might change them! At night I spoke on the fifteenth chapter of Luke, explaining it. Afterwards I asked those who had talked with me to remain. They were not all present; eight, however, remained. God has evidently been at work in their hearts. One (Tom) I almost hope is a Christian. He says, 'My heart does not feel as it did. It was all dark before, but now it is different. To-day, when you preached about Christ coming to save the lost, it made me cry. I thought, I am a lost sinner, and Christ has come to save me.' Bela seems much concerned. I never have seen deeper and more earnest and anxious attention than I have seen on the faces of many to-day. As I walked out after this morning's service to find a place of quiet and retirement, I met one native Christian and a native who had been out to the bush to pray. The native was much concerned and had asked to be taught. He was one who had been to hear me once or twice before. I sat down on the grass and tried to show him the way to Christ.

"I visited Mango's town a day or two ago and spoke to them about Christ. The king was just about buying another wife; his wives were all dead but one. I told him one was enough, and tried to persuade him to turn from heathenism unto God. He said he believed he would not get another wife now. Perhaps he would buy a slave-woman.

"*February* 27.—This has been a day of joy and grief—joy because God's work is prospering, but I was made to grieve because I find that the devil was hard at work, too. I paid a visit to M'Lachlan (trader), on the other side. He spoke of putting a factory right among my people—a *rum-shop* to ruin the mission work. I plead for God and his cause with all the strength I could. May God break the teeth of his enemies! At night also in the town there was a drunken frolic while we were at meeting, and one of the men who had been most concerned about his soul was in it. Rum was bought from the traders. So the devil works. At night, however, we had a good meeting, and for this in my heart I can thank God. Thirteen or fourteen stayed in after the meeting was over to ask and learn the way to Christ. Some of them I had talked with before. Five women stayed this time. Some of them seemed to be a good deal concerned.

Oh, I trust God will yet convert multitudes of these people to himself.

"*March* 2.—The interest of those who have been inquiring the way to God seems unabated. About fifteen stayed in to-night to inquire and hear about God. I appointed Saturday afternoon for them all to come. The people of Hanje and Aje are coming out encouragingly to church. My house is wellnigh finished with the exception of the floors.

"*Saturday*, March 4.—This afternoon I had appointed to meet the inquirers. There were fourteen or fifteen present beside the Christians. I talked to them long and tried to explain the way to Christ. I talked to a full house to-night on 'Behold the Lamb of God.' I feel quite weary to-night, and am glad of it, from trying to serve Christ. I have walked about six miles and discoursed four times to-day.

"*Sabbath*, March 5.—This morning I preached to about one hundred people on 'Jesus stood and cried,' etc. I had much freedom in thought and word and illustration. In the afternoon prayer-meeting I spoke a little on 'Christ a propitiation for our sins.' To-night I discoursed on the terrible catalogue of heathen sins in the first chapter of

Romans. The people said, 'This is all true; we commit them all.' I talked with Isanga, Ebuma, Ihuba, Bela, Beduka and Bomani. These all, except Beduka, had some most encouraging things about them. If in another land and among a more enlightened people, their answers would make me think them Christians. I cannot tell; God knoweth. Tom also some days since gave some encouraging evidence of a change of heart.

"*Monday*, March 6.—This day I am run down with the work of yesterday and Saturday, and felt unable to do anything. But about noon the natives brought me word that Williams, a trader on the other side of the river, had died. I took boat and boatmen and went over. I found Captain Finley there, of the Gordon's schooner. Mr. Williams had died on board the schooner, and Captain Finley had already buried him. The natives had dug the grave with their hands, and a picket fence was put around it. He died without a thought of death, and I suppose had not a hope to light the grave. I tried to urge the captain to be ready also when he should be called to go, but his hardened heart turned off the subject like steel. It must be hard to die alone on the coast of Africa, unless the hope of better things beyond cheer the darkness, and then nothing might be considered easier. I am feverish to-night and a good deal unwell."

From Benita, Mr. Paull wrote, March 12, 1865, to his missionary friends Mr. and Mrs. De Heer: "Please accept many thanks for both your kind letters. I now look for my Corisco mail almost as anxiously as for my American mails, particularly since the American one for the two last times has been playing me false. It seems a long time since I saw you, but I trust it will not be many weeks till I will be among you for a little while. Christian fellowship is hard to give up. The communion of saints may well be precious to us now, for it is one of the things that will last for ever. There will be so many things, however, to add to its sweetness in heaven that we shall scarcely be able to recognize it as the communion of saints which we enjoyed on earth. This is good, but that will be infinitely better. It is well that we are not able here to realize all its excellence and preciousness, else earth would seem to us like a dreary journey through a wintry night, and we should mourn like doves until the time would come when we might fly away and join the dear company. I thank you heartily for the prayers that I know you send up on my behalf. The prayers of friends seem to me to have done more for me than anything·else in this world. The prayers, too, that have gone up for God's blessing on this station have, I trust, been answered at least in some measure. There have been several asking how they may find Christ, and some of them, I trust, have learned the way to him. I wrote you by the last mail of two who were asking the way to God. On the Sabbath evening after the mail went to Corisco several others began to inquire, and since that others, until some fifteen or eighteen have been to speak with me about 'the trouble in their hearts.' I have talked much with them and labored much to make the way to Jesus plain. Some of them, I trust, have found it, and are resting in him. How the sweet story of Jesus dying for our sins melts the heart! Most of these young men say, 'It did not trouble our hearts to know about God and heaven and hell, but when you told us about Jesus coming down and dying for our sins, then our hearts troubled us.' I rejoice greatly that God is doing something for his own glory, and I long and pray that he will yet work mightily all along this coast. I think in my heart I would desire to glorify him, but surely I have never in my life felt myself to be such a worthless, miserable atom in creation as within the last three or four weeks. But my joy is that God does not need the help of any man; he will work himself, after all, and leave us to look on.

"I have had quite an attack of fever in the last week, though I am entirely over it now. I suppose I did not follow my dear sister's advice, or I would not perhaps have had it. A week ago on Saturday I walked up the river, preaching in the towns, and then preaching twice on Sabbath, which proved to be a little more than I ought to have done. I hope wisdom will come by experience. I am sure I want to live if I can do anything for Africa. A young trader died last week. He has gone to his account. He died without a thought of death. I fear he had a dreary entrance into eternity.

"I hope it will not be long until we may speak face to face. With much love to both, affectionately, your brother,

"GEO. PAULL."

In a letter to his brother James, dated "Benita River Station, March 11, 1865," after expressing his affliction in the loss of the American mail which went down to the bottom of the sea in the steamer,

which sunk shortly after leaving Liverpool for
Africa, Mr. Paull writes: "I am greatly rejoiced
that God has sent me to labor among the mainland
tribes. If there are any privations connected with
it, I take it as high honor that he puts me to bear
them. If there be any good done, from my heart
I think I can say that I desire the glory to be his,
and I have high hopes that he will yet accomplish
much for his own glory here. Since I last wrote
home God has done many things to gladden my
heart. On Sabbath evening three weeks ago, after
feelings of great depression, and a deep sense of
utter helplessness and worthlessness in the world, I
preached on John iii. 16, 17: 'For God so loved
the world,' etc. And God was pleased, I trust, to
bless it to the good of some of these poor heathen.
Some had seemed thoughtful before, and many were
so earnestly attentive to the truth that I thought
it good to ask that all might remain after the bene-
diction who were anxious to know more of Christ and
of the way to him. Quite a number remained,
five or six of whom complained of their hearts
troubling them on account of sin. Since that fifteen or eighteen have come to my little native hut
to speak with me about their souls. Some of them
are really and deeply concerned, and some of them

I think have found Christ, and are believing in him. One young man who had been a great sinner before, now says that he hates his old life, and does not wish to live it again.   He says : ' My heart not feel now like it did ; when you preach to-day about Christ coming to save the lost, I feel I be lost sinner, and Christ he save me, and it make me weep.'   With but few exceptions they never heard the gospel until last November, when I made a trip here, and left Mbata as a Scripture reader.   Since I have been here I have tried morning and evening to instruct them as to the evil of their hearts and their utterly lost and helpless condition, but especially pointing them to Christ, and trying to open up to them his fullness and freeness and willingness to save.   I have long felt that Christ is everything to sinners, and preaching anything else is of no use. And it is wonderful how the simple love of Christ is able to melt even the heathen heart.   Almost every one that came to me said, ' We heard of God and heaven and hell from the Scripture reader, but it did not trouble us ; but when you told us about Christ coming into the world and dying for our sins, then our hearts trouble us much.'   If only one soul be saved from heathenish darkness and eternal death, and be made an heir of glory by words that God shall enable me to speak, then I shall have reason to bless him for ever that he has sent me to Africa.

"I sat to-night musing about home, and thinking how delightful it would be to spend an evening with you all, and especially a Sabbath evening, as you are gathered around the fire. My life is now altogether without those comforts of home and friends, and I scarcely ever see the face of a white man, except it be an occasional trader, since I came here. But I am far happier here, feeling that I am doing something for God, than I have ever been at home, where I have often felt that my days were idly, almost sinfully, floating away. It is not ease or comfort that can make us happy: it is only the feeling that we are redeeming the time for God that can give us peace. I do not know whether my life in Africa will be long or short, nor does that give me any trouble, so I be sure that my heart is wholly fixed on Christ. This is all that need give me any concern. But whatever the length of my life may be, I trust God will enable me to give it all for Africa. Every earthly thing is very small when eternity opens up before us, and we are wrong if we do not always keep eternity in the foreground. If it make us solemn, all the better; we have no right to be anything else but solemn; for surely it is a solemn thing to live and still more so to die; so that living or dying, we ought to be solemn. Our hearts are apt to plead for a little mirth and levity, and they say these things will not harm us; but they only tell us lies; they would ruin us if they could; the Scriptures call them ' deceitful above all things, and desperately wicked.' I am sure we have no enemy so bad or so dangerous as our own hearts.

" I have not yet got into my new house, but hope to do so shortly. There is a delightful breeze always fanning the rooms and a fine view over the sea, that strangely contrasts with my present abode, which is hemmed in with plantain trees all around the town, so that the little houses can scarcely be seen, and the house has no windows to admit the breeze. I suppose I would be able to get some monkey meat if I wished it. One of the men shot one the other day, but I did not get to see it till he had burned all the hair off it except the tail. This is the way they cook them, with the skin on. It was a little red one—red as a fox. There are great numbers of them in the bush. The same man also speared a shark in the mouth of the river, and another shot a deer on the beach near town.　There is abundance of game, but the guns they have are so worthless they rarely kill anything.

"The last mail brought me a paper from Mr. Thompson, of Glasgow, which says there are many rumors and a good prospect of peace in America. I sincerely hope it may be so, and that this sorrowful war will soon be ended and the country again united."

To his mother:

"Corisco, April 10, 1865.

"Your letters and one from James reached me yesterday.　These brought me the only tidings from home that I have had for three months.　The letters which you wrote me in November and December, I suppose, are in the bottom of the English Channel, a loss which I deplore more than you can tell.　I see by one of my last letters that Cousin Thomas Foster has gone to rest.　I hope he has gone to the land from which, if we once enter, we go no more out.　Uncle and Aunt B. have had heavy shadows drifting over them these late years. I trust when the sun shines again its beams will be the purer and brighter for the cloudy days. You see from the date of my letter that I am now at Corisco, though I expect to go back to my Benita home in a day or two. I came down to attend communion, the mission-meeting and meeting of Presbytery. My stay here has been very pleasant and refreshing after ten weeks' absence from white faces, and Corisco too seems like a home, though my own station among the Kombes has a hold on my heart which makes the thought of going back to it very pleasant. The interest among the people there in reference to the things that make for their peace, causes me to wish to be among them again, with the hope that the divine spark will be re-kindled and many more inquire the way to Zion. I wish and pray that, with a heart undivided by any earthly thing, I may be enabled to labor in my wide field for the glory of our King and the salvation of the people.

"I had a letter from my Scotch friend, Mr. George Thompson, saying that he had sent a box of canned meats for me and Mrs. Nassau by the ship St. George. He had seen Mrs. Nassau on her way home through Scotland. The meats have arrived. I am glad the box from Africa reached home and gave you some pleasure. I hope some day to send you a larger one. I had hoped this mail would bring us tidings of an honorable peace, but the day still seems distant.

18

"I do not know any thought more comforting and pleasant than that of dwelling for ever in the ages to come with the meek and quiet in spirit—a harmonious and happy family, undisturbed by passion, and filled and permeated with eternal and unchanging love. Those who have most of love in them upon earth are nearest to heaven, and love grows in us just in proportion as selfishness and worldliness dies.

"My health in my new home has been wonderfully good except one or two little touches of fever which are common to all, and which come and go in a day or two; but I came down looking much better, the missionaries tell me, than when I went away. I hope I shall be spared in Africa many years yet to come.

"*April* 13.—Started for Benita again this morning with two boats loaded with furniture, goods and provisions. The moon came up like a ball of fire, at 7 o'clock, and we sailed along in the beautiful moonlight, reaching Benita about 12 o'clock at night. Many of the people came with their hearty welcome and helped us unload the boat. I slept in my new house for the first time, on a mattress thrown on the floor.

"*April* 14.—Breakfasted on some provisions

Mrs. Mackey sent along, my table a chest and the floor my chair. Very busy putting down matting, setting up bedsteads, wardrobe and book-case and unpacking stores. The people in the house all day in crowds, some helping, others looking on, all seeming glad.

"*Sabbath*, April 15.—This has been a good and glad day. Discoursed three times in my new house to good, serious and attentive audiences— morning on 'Blind Bartimeus,' afternoon, 'Ye will not come unto me,' evening 'What think ye of Christ?'— chiefly endeavoring to hold up Christ in his mediatorial work, urging all to accept of him. I seem to feel that God's spirit is present with us yet, as I trust he was before I went away.

"*April* 20.—Kema's daughter seems to have become really serious. I see her always present at prayers morning and night, whether it rains or not —often the only woman present. It is a strange feature here that the women are the very last to become interested in spiritual things."

We now come to Mr. Paull's last letter, which was finished by Mr. Mackey, at his request. It was addressed from Benita River Station, April 17, 1865, to his brother James:

"My indebtedness is to you this time. I feel

very grateful to you and mother and Lizzie for having kept me so well informed of the progress of things at home. The wide gap that the loss of two months' mails made was no fault of yours, but one of those providences which come divinely ordered, doing their work and leaving us to wonder why they came. I wrote to mother and Lizzie while I was at Corisco. I am so far from the 'central point' it is necessary to take every opportunity lest I get to send no letter at all; so my dates will be very irregular, though I hope to get a letter to you by every mail. I write this now, as I shall be obliged to go to Corisco again in about two weeks, and I wish to leave it there for the mail. I would not go if I did not feel that it was important to be there on the arrival of Mr. Clark and the departure of Mr. Mackey, so that we may consult all together about the interests and prospects of our work. A sea voyage of over one hundred miles (there and back) in an open boat, and almost constant sun or rain, is not a very delightful undertaking. The chief part of my work, however, will require boating up and down the coast, but the journeys will neither be so hard nor so long as that to Corisco.

"We had a meeting of Presbytery while I was

at Corisco, and divided the church, making arrangements to organize the second one here; so my charge will now lie north of Cape St. John—a point about halfway between this and Corisco—and extends as far north above this as I am able to go. I hope we shall soon have a station here and there like a line of beacon-lights, all along the coast, pouring out their bright light for the safety and salvation of Africa's bewildered ones. Within two or three months the church will be organized here, and one of the missionaries will be up to help me at the organization. My visit to Corisco was a pleasant one; it was good to be among the missionaries after a tolerably long absence, and they greeted me with warm welcomes.

"*April* 18.—I laid my matting on the study to-day, put up the book-case, wardrobe and bedstead, so that the room begins to look somewhat comfortable, at least much better than my quondam home in the native hut. And as I hope to make some more additions of furniture after a while, I need not envy any one his comforts.

"I left Ngambalonda at Corisco, but have another boy (Ijubi) who lives with me and sleeps in the next room. He is one of those who were inquiring before I went to Corisco; and I hope he is a Christian. Every night I hear him offering low but private prayers to God in his native tongue—and it is by no means a small comfort and delight here to hear a heathen boy begin to pray. There is the same good attendance and attention that there was before I went away. Those who were interested come regularly and faithfully to morning and evening prayers, and to every meeting for prayer, although some of them have more than a quarter of a mile to walk, sometimes in pitchy darkness, and almost trembling for fear of the leopards. I hope in the last day it will be found that they have washed their robes and made them white in the blood of the Lamb. Every one who is received into the church here must be received with fear and trembling, for if they stand and keep from open sin, it can only be because they are upheld by the most amazing grace of God. There are a thousand earthly helps to bolster a Christian up in a civilized land; but here there is scarcely a single prop. A healthy moral sentiment in the community is one of the greatest helps to Christians at home, but here there is no moral sentiment at all. The reins are all thrown loose, and they may and do commit the vilest sins as freely as they like. Imagine what a people must be without government, without laws, without religion, without morals!

"*April* 20.—To-night the rain patters down heavily on the roof, and the sound is not unpleasant, but has rather a soothing effect when one is under good shelter. But the thunder bursts loudly overhead, and the red lightning darts in at every crack. A bamboo house is by no means a tight structure, for it is easy to read by the light which pours in through the cracks, when the doors and window-shutters are all closed. But this does not hinder it from being a comfortable place to live in, for the air also finds entrance at the openings; and it would be difficult to get along without plenty of fresh air.

" I went out in the bush to-day to see if I could find some fresh meat. In the bush, only a little distance away, we found deer tracks almost as plenty as rabbit tracks around a thicket at home, and the fresh tracks of what is said to be a wild cow, as though she had just leaped by; and it seemed to be a perfect play-ground for elephants, for the traces of them were all around, where they had rubbed on the trees and put their huge feet in the mud. We came across about a dozen monkeys in the top of a tree cracking nuts. I would have been willing to forego my prejudices and eat a piece of one of them, as the natives and white men on the coast eat them, and esteem them excellent food. But if I ever knew anything about hunting I have forgotten it now ; for they all slipped away through the tops of the trees, and we came home without anything. I had Upingalo with me, and another native. The monkeys go in great droves usually, leaping along from tree-top to tree-top like squirrels, and they may be seen almost any morning or evening by a short walk."

Here Mr. Paull's pen ceases its work. The Rev. Mr. Mackey continues :

"This letter was written so far before your brother's last illness. When on his death-bed at my house he requested me to take it from his portfolio, finish and forward it to you, in case he should be called away.

"Your brother George has run his earthly race, he has finished his course, and he has gone to receive his crown. He died on Sabbath morning, May 14, a little before 11 o'clock, while the congregation was worshiping in the church close by.

"Your brother was a most faithful and devoted laborer in the cause of Christ. The members of our mission esteemed him most highly as a Christian brother and fellow‑laborer. The people around his station on the mainland loved him and received his teachings with gladness. I feel that I have lost a personal friend. My dear wife mourns his loss as that of a brother. We do not repine or rebel against the will of God. He who does all things well has afflicted us and you, but it is done in love.   Yours sincerely,

"JAMES L. MACKEY."

An extract from a letter written a short time before his death so well expresses his views and feelings in entering upon the new station at Benita, that we give it here, though not in its chronological order:

"To go and live among the mainland tribes and declare unto them the gospel—is not this high honor? For some time I have had charge of the out-stations extending along the coast for about fifty miles, and I have visited them by boat, but now I go to live among them and give my time wholly to the work. If ever I wished to live it is now, when my heart has hope that I may yet do something for God and something for Africa. A peculiar confidence has gradually been growing stronger within me that God will yet give me grace to do something that shall be for his glory. Thus God is gradually opening for me the way I have so much desired to go, and I count it goodness and mercy in him. For years I have besought the Lord for just the thing he seems to be giving me now, and he has led me to it along a path in many respects different from my expectations. His faithfulness hitherto has made me strong in the confidence that by his grace he will keep me from falling unto the end. My darkness and my temptations which pressed so sorely on me for many months have passed away, and I cannot doubt that they have left me stronger in the Lord, and have introduced me more fully into the precious and abiding love of Christ. If I be not deceived, there is growing within me a firmer resolve to glorify God and to be unreservedly given to him. His character has been growing daily more beautiful to me, and thoughts of his infinite excellence fill my heart at times fuller than it can hold. Do not fear, my friends, that any prospect of earthly happiness will turn me away from the work to which God has called me. God is too merciful to suffer that. I count it better a thousand times to die than to desert my 'post.' "

This noble faith in God and devotion to the

great work of preaching the gospel to the sable tribes of Africa affords a sublime illustration of the power of divine grace in conquering all natural attachment to the world and bringing all the powers of the soul into the obedience of Christ.

Dr. Nassau, after giving a full account of Mr. Paull's illness from his return from Benita to Corisco to the day before his death, writes: "On Saturday, 13th, Mr. Mackey asked him whether in the face of an early death he had any regrets for having come to Africa. He decidedly and warmly said, 'No, no, no;' and added that his only sorrow was for the grief that his relatives and friends would feel. Late in the afternoon, as Mr. De Heer was going back to his station, Mr. Paull rose up suddenly in his bed and said, 'Oh, brother de Heer, I am so nervous.' Mr. De Heer reminded him that there was rest for the weary. 'Oh yes; if I could only fully realize that!' How sweet in weakness to derive strength from Christ and rest leaning on the arm of our Beloved. 'Yes, I long for that rest.' As they pressed hands for the last time, Mr. De Heer said, 'If no more on earth, brother, we trust we shall meet in that better world.' 'Pray much for me, and ask all to pray for me,' was the reply."

Dr. Nassau continues: "In the twilight of the evening (I fanning him) he said, 'Repeat that hymn.' None had been spoken of, and I asked which. He replied, 'Just as I am.' A little after 9 o'clock he moaned, seemingly not intending to speak audibly, 'Lord Jesus, don't cast me away. Such clouds and darkness on my mind.' 'Has there been to-day?' 'Yes, for two weeks.' 'While you have been sick here?' 'Yes.' 'He says He is light. There is light there, though we do not see it.' 'True.' 'And Christian in his darkness felt a hand, though he saw none. The grace that availed for the heathen you preached to at Benita avails for you.' 'That is so, that is so.' 'We sinners all need the same grace. "Him that cometh unto me I will in no wise cast out."' '*In no wise, in no wise.*' I prayed, then, arising, said, 'He is a covenant-keeping God; he does not break covenants.' 'No.' After an interval he added, 'Lord, pity me, pity, pity, pity.' He lay quietly much of the former part of the night, but not asleep, for often I heard scarcely audible words of ejaculatory prayer, and expressions like, 'O Father, dear Saviour,' etc. Just at midnight, when he was lying so quietly that I thought him almost asleep, he said in a low voice, as if speaking to himself, 'Jesus can make a dying bed feel soft as downy pillows are.' I carried it on, 'While on his breast I lean my head,' and he finished the fourth line, 'And breathe my life out sweetly there.'

"At one time on Sabbath morning I thought death had come when he uttered, in a drawn out, slow manner, 'Lord Jesus, receive my spirit!' Later still he spoke more distinctly, 'Saviour, Saviour, give me more light, more trust in thee.' One of his last utterances before he died was, 'I wish to lay myself at the feet of Jesus, and to feel that Jesus is my all.' The loved friend felt Jesus with him before he actually was ushered into the enjoyment of the Sabbath above. I am sure that God lifted that painfully obscuring veil, and showed your son and brother his face while yet in the valley. He could not desert one who in every walk and conversation of life had honored him."

Thus the Christian missionary, whose heart God so strongly inclined to preach his precious gospel to the perishing heathen in Africa, has gone to rest in glory, honored and beloved by all who knew him. His body sleeps in the beautiful mission cemetery, at Corisco, awaiting the resurrection morn when them that sleep in Jesus shall God bring with him. Two oleanders, planted by loving hands, one at the head and the other at the foot of his grave, now bloom monthly in fragrant beauty, emblematic of that immortal bloom which awaits the raised body in the celestial country. His spirit, so ardent in devotion here, I doubt not is among the most seraphic of the spirits of the just made perfect, now striking its golden harp in notes of praise to redeeming love. His bright moral image, now reflecting more perfectly the likeness of his Saviour, still lives in the memory of those who knew him on earth, preaching most impressively the great duty of love and fidelity to Christ as the only true preparation for the crown of life.

A marble monument marks his tomb, with the emblem of a *cross and crown*, and the inscription:

Rev. GEORGE PAULL.

Born Feb. 3, 1837.

Died May 14, 1865.

Also I heard the voice of the Lord saying, Whom shall
I send and who will go for us? Then said he,
Here am I, send me.—Isaiah vii. 8.

Dr. Nassau, on visiting Benita, wrote, "My heart sank with heaviness for the breach that the Lord has made upon us. When the news of Mr. Paull's death reached Benita the people trembled

GRAVE OF MR. PAULL.

p. 286.

—the native word means to be agitated exceedingly—and wailing was heard through all the towns as when a great man of their own tribe dies. I found that he had obtained a deep and firm hold on the people's affections. Those who were seeking Christ told me mournfully of their sorrow for their missionary's death, and wistfully asked whether another would come. I think I may count ten as hopefully Christians, and as many more as sincere inquirers, and others whose heathenish habits are modified and who respect the Sabbath and other institutions of religion."

If the death of Mr. Paull brought sadness to the mission circle in Africa, and called forth the wail of the heathen in their towns, so did it bring sore grief to hearts in America. Yet the grief of those who loved him was tempered by the knowledge of his godly life and blessed estate, and by the warm words of those who knew him well. Letters of condolence from men eminent in the Church, resolutions of Presbytery, and the poetic tribute of affectionate admiration, bore witness to the regard in which he was held, but will not be needed by those who have read the record of his life. This plain record will enable them to form a just estimate of his character.

I have permitted this noble young Christian missionary to entertain and instruct my readers by his letters, addressed in the usual freedom of correspondence to his relatives and intimate friends, and not designed by him for the public eye. Had they known him personally, they would not wonder that I should take the labor of transcribing them for their benefit. May God imbue them with a double portion of that Christian spirit which animated the heart of his missionary to Corisco!

To the young let me say, would you possess a lofty Christian record on earth and an unfading crown in heaven, commit your souls to God in early life with the earnest and daily prayer of the Apostle to the Gentiles, " Lord, what wilt thou have me to do ?" Bring your young hearts to Christ in loving faith and fervent devotion to his church. Cherish that true concern for the perishing heathen which made Mr. Paull so happy in preaching the gospel even in Africa. If you have his faith and zeal in the cause, though you be not called to labor and lay your bodies in Africa or India, you may nevertheless share in the glory to be revealed when " They that are wise shall shine as the brightness of the firmament, and they that turn many to righteousness as the stars for ever and ever."